TILL SUDDEN DEATH DO US PART

A Selection of Recent Titles by Simon R. Green

The Ishmael Jones Mysteries

THE DARK SIDE OF THE ROAD *
DEAD MAN WALKING *
VERY IMPORTANT CORPSES *
DEATH SHALL COME *
INTO THE THINNEST OF AIR *
MURDER IN THE DARK *
TILL SUDDEN DEATH DO US PART *

The Secret History Series

PROPERTY OF A LADY FAIRE
FROM A DROOD TO A KILL
DR DOA
MOONBREAKER
NIGHT FALL

The Nightside Series

JUST ANOTHER JUDGEMENT DAY
THE GOOD, THE BAD, AND THE UNCANNY
A HARD DAY'S KNIGHT
THE BRIDE WORE BLACK LEATHER

* *available from Severn House*

TILL SUDDEN DEATH DO US PART

Simon R. Green

Severn House Large Print
London & New York

This first large print edition published 2019
in Great Britain and the USA by
SEVERN HOUSE PUBLISHERS LTD of
Eardley House, 4 Uxbridge Street, London W8 7SY.
First world regular print edition published 2019 by
Severn House Publishers Ltd.

British Library Cataloguing in Publication Data
A CIP catalogue record for this title is available from the British Library.

ISBN-13: 9780727892379

Severn House Publishers support the Forest Stewardship Council™
[FSC™], the leading international forest certification organisation. All
our titles that are printed on FSC certified paper carry the FSC logo.

MIX
Paper from
responsible sources
FSC
www.fsc.org   FSC® C013056

Typeset by Palimpsest Book Production Ltd.,
Falkirk, Stirlingshire, Scotland.
Printed and bound in Great Britain by
T J International, Padstow, Cornwall.

Call me Ishmael. Ishmael Jones.

We're all haunted by our own past. By the people we used to be, the things we did or left undone. All the people whose lives we touched, for better or worse. The memories that stir in the early hours of the morning when we can't sleep. We are all the product of all the different people we've been. Even the ones we don't remember.

In 1963, a shooting star streaked across the night sky before falling to an English field. Or, to put it another way, an alien starship from God knows where crash-landed in the middle of the night, unseen and unsuspected. The impact killed all the crew but one, who was rewritten by the ship's transformation machines, so he could live as a human among humans until rescue arrived. But help never came. And the transformation machines were so damaged by the crash they wiped all memories of who and what I used to be, before I was human. Before I came to myself, stumbling confused and alone across a ploughed field in the early hours of the morning.

Born into the present, with an unknown past.

I've spent my life as a succession of different people, working for any number of secret organizations, because only they have the resources to hide a man who hasn't aged a day since 1963 from an increasingly curious and surveillance-heavy world. These days, I work for the Organization; solving cases of the weird and uncanny with the help of my delightfully human partner, Penny Belcourt. Protecting the world from all the monsters that threaten it.

But . . . am I a man dreaming he used to be an alien, or an alien dreaming he's a man? The difference is important. Because after all these years, I think the alien is waking up.

One

The Past is Always Looking Over My Shoulder

When I looked into the mirror that morning, I didn't recognize the face looking back at me. It was my face, but it didn't mean anything to me. I stood there in Penny's bathroom, my hand reaching for the shaving gel just like any other morning; but suddenly my heart was hammering in my chest and I couldn't seem to get my breath. And then the human face faded away, and something else looked back at me from out of the mirror. A face that wasn't a face, that wasn't human in any way, but still something in me recognized it. It was the face I had before I was born, before I was a man. A nightmare shape, a thing of horror, that usually I only glimpsed in dreams, right before I woke up screaming. My old self, before the transformation machines had their way with me. The alien face stared steadily back at me like a long-buried memory that wasn't content to stay forgotten any longer. Like some imprisoned beast, testing the bars of its cage to see how strong they were.

And in that moment I didn't feel like a man any more; as though all of me was just a passing thought in something much bigger and much older.

The alien shape vanished, and my human face stared back out of the mirror again. I knew it immediately, the other face gone like a half-remembered nightmare. I looked scared. It took me a while, before my hands were steady enough to pick up the shaving gel and the disposable razor. But I've always prided myself on my self-control. That I would always be able to do what I needed to do, to survive. Ever since I first woke up in a world I didn't know, haunted by a past I couldn't remember.

I had a right to be scared. Because if whoever or whatever I used to be was finally waking from its long sleep, I had no idea what that old self would make of me. All I could be sure of was that it was alien; that it wouldn't think or feel or act in any way human. Perhaps to that self, Ishmael Jones was nothing more than a mask it had chosen to wear for a time, to be tossed aside as no longer needed.

Perhaps I wasn't even a mask. Just a cage, whose bars weren't as strong as I'd thought.

'You cut yourself shaving,' said Penny, peering out from behind the *Financial Times* as I sat down opposite her at the breakfast table. 'I don't think I've ever seen you do that before. And the scab is golden, just like your blood.'

I brushed vaguely at my face, with an entirely steady hand. 'It'll be gone before I have to go out. How are your investments looking today?'

'You had the bad dream again last night,' she said, folding the paper and putting it to one side. 'Did I wake you?'

4

'Yes. And you didn't even notice. Do you remember anything?'

'No,' I said.

She nodded, and addressed herself to the plate of food in front of her. Penny was a great believer in starting the day on a full stomach. Which for her meant a full English fried breakfast of sausages, bacon, eggs and hot buttered toast; or as she liked to call it, a cholesterol special. I think you have to be in pretty good shape already just to survive something like that. Penny attacked her pile of crispy bacon with great enthusiasm, while I poured myself a large black coffee. I am not a morning person. My stomach doesn't even want to know about food at such an ungodly hour. I'm not even that keen on conversation. By long agreement, neither of us commented on the other's chosen lifestyle. Of such small compromises are relationships forged.

It was the weekend, and once again I was staying at Penny's little flat, in a very select area of London. I don't like to fall into predictable patterns, it makes me too easy to track down. But it meant so much to her, that I spent as much time with her as I could.

Penny was a glamorous presence, even first thing in the morning, with no make-up and her dark hair piled carelessly on top of her head. She was wearing her favourite battered old dressing gown, of a colour so faded it was barely a suggestion. Her dark eyes flashed merrily whenever she glanced at me, and her every smile warmed my heart.

I didn't tell Penny about my experience with

5

the mirror. Though whether I was protecting her or me, I wasn't sure. I wouldn't have known what to say anyway. Human language just doesn't have the words or concepts to describe what I saw. Penny could tell there was something wrong, but she knew better than to press me. Perhaps the secret to a successful relationship is deciding which secrets to share.

I nursed my coffee while Penny demolished enough food to stun a restaurant critic, until finally she pushed her empty plate aside with a loud satisfied sound, and fixed me with a determined look.

'You need a good walk,' she said briskly. 'Something to stir the blood and shake loose the cobwebs. Anywhere special you feel like going?'

'Soho,' I said. The word pushed its way past my lips before I'd even considered it. But the moment I said the name, I knew that nowhere else would do. 'I haven't been back there in ages, but I feel the need to visit the old place again. If only to see how much it's changed.'

'How long ago are we talking about?' said Penny.

'I came to Soho in the sixties,' I said. 'Back then, it was the best place for someone like me to hide in plain sight.'

Penny clapped her hands delightedly. 'You knew London in the Swinging Sixties? Carnaby Street and the King's Road? Groovy fashions and flower power, happenings and be-ins and all that?'

I looked at her, and she shrugged.

'I love sixties movies.'

'I was that hippie,' I said. 'I suppose most of what I remember is probably gone now.'

'We should definitely go and look,' said Penny.

And that was how we ended up walking through London's Soho on a bright and cheerful Saturday morning. Strolling through the crowded streets arm in arm, just like any other young couple taking in the sights. I remembered the names of the streets, but it seemed like everything else had changed. The sunlight made everything look new and fresh, even though we were in a part of the city that dated back to Roman times. But then, London has always been good at reinventing itself to meet the needs of the present.

Back in the sixties, Soho was an urban jungle. Blazing with bright neon and full of all kinds of attractions, designed to lure the prey to the predators. The narrow streets were lined with nightclubs and restaurants, fashionable shops and shops selling fashions, strippers and satirists and bars packed full of characters. Let the good times roll and never look back; so you wouldn't see what was creeping up on you. You could find dreams and delight alongside dangers for the unwary . . . and what a time it was, to be young and careless.

By the seventies most of that was gone, the sense of adventure replaced by wall-to-wall sleaze. Sex cinemas, sex shops, and clip joints where under-dressed hostesses pressured the punters into buying them cheap champagne at extortionate prices, while promising favours they were never going to deliver. Above the sex shops lurked discreet little rooms, where discerning gentlemen could spend time with ladies like the lovely Vera, who could be very understanding. What the punters never knew was that there were three lovely Veras doing eight-hour shifts so the bed was always warm.

'You've got that look on your face,' said Penny. 'The one that says you're remembering a time when things were different.'

'The sixties were different,' I said. 'But it wasn't all Summer of Love and the Age of Aquarius, *International Times* and *Oz* magazine. That was the dream. There were good times to be had, but often people went home to cold-water flats and shared toilets, race riots and political corruption, and tiny black-and-white television sets with only two channels. No central heating and the only radiator was coin-operated, so in the winter it got so cold you piled coats on top of blankets to keep warm at night, and you woke to frost on the inside of your window in pretty fern patterns.'

'It's like listening to someone from a Charles Dickens novel,' said Penny. 'I tend to forget, until you remind me, how old you really are. Just as well I've always had a thing for older men.'

I looked at her. 'I won't ask.'

'Best not to,' Penny said briskly. 'What were you doing in Soho, in the sixties?'

'I was working for Department Y. The first secret group I ever belonged to.'

'Y?' said Penny.

8

'I don't know,' I said solemnly. 'It was a secret.'
She punched me in the arm, which was what
I deserved.

'What name were you using, back then?' said
Penny, slipping her arm through mine again to
show I was forgiven.

I shook my head firmly. 'I've used many names
down the years, but right now I'm Ishmael Jones
and only Ishmael Jones. Because I don't care to
remember some of the people I had to be.'

'All right,' said Penny. 'Can you at least tell
me who you were working with, back then?
Anyone I'd know?'

'I doubt it,' I said. 'None of them are part of
the scene any more. There was Lady Patricia, the
supernatural socialite. The cool blonde with
the icy heart, and a sense for danger that was
never wrong. Doctor Alien; who turned out to
be neither. Fabulous Freddie, and the Acid
Sorcerer. It was a time for weird names and
colourful personalities. And then of course, there
was the Groovy Ghoul.'

'Was he one of the good guys?' said Penny.

'Hard to tell,' I said. 'In Department Y we
worked cases like the Downing Street
Dopplegangers, Springheel Jack, the Metal Mods
and Revolution Nine. It was an extravagant time,
and even our secrets were gaudy things. We
thought we were living in an age of wonders,
that would see the mind's true liberation through
acid trips, mantras, and radical politics. The
reality was rather different.'

I looked down the street before us, and the
bustling crowds disappeared as my memory

9

showed me a vision of the way things used to be.

This was the street where Springheel Jack was brought to bay at last. A dark gargoyle figure in his gas mask and horns, glowing eyes and fiery breath, and a long flapping cape. He brandished his cane defiantly, and flecks of blood flew on the air from the fresh gore that soaked the heavy silver head. Jack had been busy, striking down working girls with the wrath of his unforgiving god. Lady Patricia smiled at him, cool and sophisticated as always, dressed in her pink hunting outfit and calfskin jodhpurs. No one paid any attention. People wore stranger things in public, back then. She aimed her long-barrelled pistol with a perfectly steady hand as Springheel Jack charged down the street towards her, screaming muffled threats and obscenities from behind his mask, dodging and ducking the bullets Lady Patricia fired at him. She stood her ground and kept firing. Until Jack was close enough for me to step out of the side alley and club him to the ground with a single blow.

I ripped off his mask and horns, to reveal a perfectly ordinary face. No one I knew, but that was probably the point. It's always the ones who feel neglected and overlooked who feel the need to make an exhibition of themselves in public. Jack tried to get to his feet again, and Lady Patricia shot him through the kneecap with her last bullet. And that was that.

The scene changed, as memory showed me another time. I was chasing Toby Slaughter down the same street, with Lady Patricia right behind me. Toby plunged into a crowded street market and there were sudden screams as people scattered, trying to get out of his way. Toby cut viciously about him with his gleaming straight razors, and blood flew on the air as men and women were thrown back into the tightly-packed food stalls. I finally ran Toby down and jumped him from behind. I slammed him to the ground, knocking the breath out of him, but he still had enough strength to put up a fight. We wrestled fiercely, until I was forced to let him go and jump back, to avoid a sweeping razor-blade that would have opened up my throat.

We were both quickly back on our feet again. The market was deserted, everyone else taken to their heels. Toby was breathing hard. I wasn't. He cut at me again and again, but I kept my distance, dodging and ducking the shining straight razors with my more than human speed and reflexes. Waiting for Lady Patricia to arrive and take the shot. But that didn't happen. I finally risked a glance back down the street, and saw Lady Patricia was still some distance back; gamely struggling along, but out of breath and out of range. I was going to have to do this myself. So I chose my moment carefully, snatched up half a melon from a nearby stall, and used it to intercept one of the razors. And while Toby hesitated, I kicked him square in the nuts. The strength of the blow lifted him up into the air, and when he crashed to the ground he'd dropped both his razors, and lost interest in anything but curling up into a ball and crying his eyes out.

I stood over him, kicking the razors out of his reach, just in case. Looking down at the man who'd killed so many children, just because he could. I wanted to kill him; but orders had come down from on high that he was to be taken alive. Toby Slaughter had aristocratic connections, under his real name. He'd probably end up in some quiet luxury nut house, to avoid embarrassing the House of Lords. Lady Patricia finally joined me, so out of breath she could barely stand up straight. And I realized for the first time that she had to be in her forties now, and no longer the bright young thing who'd been my first partner in Department Y.

'Sorry I'm a bit late, darling,' she said finally. 'Who knew the little turd could run that fast? I'm surprised he's still alive. You saw what he did to those kids.'

'You saw the orders,' I said.

'To hell with the orders,' she said, and shot Toby Slaughter in the head. She shot him twice more, just to be certain, and then lowered her gun and smiled at me. 'I have aristocratic connections too.'

'Y isn't going to be very happy about this,' I said.

She shrugged. 'It's past time I retired to my country seat and grew roses, like I always wanted to.' She looked at the dead body and shook her head. 'It's cases like this that spoiled things. It's not fun and games any more.'

The past faded away, the sixties and the seventies retreating into the mists of memory, and I

12

was back in the here and now. None of the buildings around me were in any way familiar. The ones I remembered had all been pulled down, renovated or rebuilt, in the ongoing effort to make Soho safe for tourists. The world I knew was gone. Lady Patricia retired, Doctor Alien vanished into a mirror in 1969, and the Groovy Ghoul never came back from a bad acid trip. Even Department Y was gone; swallowed up in the secret bureaucracy.

Penny could see I was affected by my memories, and jumped to an understandable misconception. 'Was this Lady Patricia more than just a partner to you?'

I smiled, and shook my head. 'No; Patricia never made any secret of the fact that she played for the other team. All jolly hockeysticks, and girls-only clubs. Which was a pretty brave stand to make, back in the sixties. In her own way, she was almost as much an outsider as I was. Which is probably why we worked so well together. After I left Department Y I drifted through half a dozen subterranean groups, of varying respectability. Fighting the good fight in the shadowy corners of the world, being the secret monster who hunted other monsters. Until finally I joined Black Heir, in the mid-eighties.

'I'd always given them lots of room before, because they specialized in cleaning up after close encounters and might just know an alien when they saw one, but in the end I decided I needed to know what they knew. In particular, whether they might know where my long-lost starship was buried. But if they did know

13

anything, it was hidden behind so many layers of security I couldn't get anywhere near it.'

'All these secret groups,' said Penny. 'All the strange people and weird happenings . . . It's like a whole other world. I can't believe I never even suspected . . .'

'A lot of people go to a lot of trouble to keep the secret world secret,' I said. 'Because most people couldn't cope with the truth. Or at least, that's the official position. I think most people are stronger than that.'

'You think they could cope with knowing about you?' said Penny.

'I wouldn't go that far,' I said. 'I have no intention of ending up in a zoo, or strapped to a dissecting table, or worst of all, on a reality TV show.'

'Still,' said Penny, 'there are groups who'd be thrilled to meet an actual extraterrestrial. You know; the saucer watchers, the true believers. Calling occupants of interplanetary craft, and all that.'

'Are you kidding? Have you met those people? Some of them are weirder than I'll ever be. And anyway; I'd only disappoint them. I'm not nearly alien enough to satisfy the real enthusiasts.'

Penny looked around her, taking in the bright open streets and the happy crowds. 'How many years has it been, since you were last here?'

'Ages,' I said. 'It really was a different world, then.'

'Is there any chance someone here might recognize you?'

'We're talking fifty years ago,' I said. 'More

than enough for people to forget a face, never mind a name. And even if someone here did think I looked familiar, they wouldn't believe I was the same man. How could I be? I'd just be someone who reminded them of someone else.'

Penny shook her head slowly. I didn't say anything. She preferred to forget that while we might look the same age, there was a gap of years between us that could never be closed. And then I turned away from her, as I was struck by a sudden feeling of being watched. Without making a big deal of it, I turned slowly in a complete circle, glancing this way and that, like any other tourist. The streets were full of people just walking along, doing normal things, and none of them seemed to be paying me or Penny any undue attention. But I still felt the subtle pressure of unseen eyes, from some hidden watcher. Developing instincts like that is part of what's kept me alive all these years. And finally I spotted the Colonel, moving slowly and remorselessly through the crowds towards us.

People hurried to get out of his way without quite realizing why they were doing it. Reacting unconsciously to his natural air of authority. The Colonel; the middleman, the public face of the Organization. The man who gave me my orders and sent me out on missions. I drew Penny's attention to the Colonel, and she glared at me accusingly.

'You didn't tell me we were coming here to meet him. You didn't even say he'd phoned.'

'He didn't,' I said.

'But he always phones first!'

15

'I know,' I said.

'This can't be anything good,' said Penny, scowling openly at the Colonel. 'Want to make a run for it?'

'I wouldn't give him the satisfaction,' I said.

We stayed where we were, and let the Colonel come to us. Standing shoulder to shoulder to present a united front to the enemy. The Colonel saw we'd spotted him, but still took his time, strolling along and refusing to be hurried. When he finally came to a halt before us he didn't smile, just nodded coolly; every inch the professional. Tall and elegant, a man in his prime and proud of it, the Colonel wore the finest three-piece suit Savile Row could provide with casual style and all his ex-military bearing. I looked at him coldly.

'The protocol is, you always phone me first; so we can agree on a meeting place. I don't like being ambushed.'

'This isn't official business,' said the Colonel, in his dry, clipped voice. He sounded a little irritated, even disturbed, at having to make such an admission. 'But, I was ordered to seek you out and speak to you, so here I am. Someone from Black Heir has reached out to the Organization, asking for a favour. Which is . . . unusual. Apparently the request originated with someone who used to know you, back when you both worked for Black Heir.'

'No one is supposed to know that person is me,' I said sharply. 'I had a different name and identity then.'

'The Organization works with a number of other secret groups,' said the Colonel. 'A certain

16

amount of shared information is therefore inevitable. People will talk, even when they know they're not supposed to. Perhaps especially because they know they're not meant to. Rest assured; your current circumstances are still secure. You still have our protection, from all forms of surveillance and official interest. Black Heir doesn't know why this retired employee of theirs is asking you for help; they just passed the message along.'

'Are you sure about that?' I said.

'As sure as we can be, in our line of work,' said the Colonel. 'This old friend of yours hasn't told anyone why he wants your help; apparently he'll only tell you that, in person.'

I considered the Colonel for a moment, choosing my words carefully. 'Does the Organization have any objections to my answering this old friend's call for help?'

'Would it make any difference if we did?' said the Colonel.

'No,' I said. 'But I like to know where I stand.'

'You have always been free to pursue your own interests,' said the Colonel. 'As long as they don't interfere with Organization business. And there's nothing in the air at the moment which requires your particular skills. Should that change, I shall of course inform you immediately.'

'I'll bear that in mind,' I said.

'Of course you will,' said the Colonel.

Penny was glaring at him coldly. 'You swore you'd keep Ishmael hidden from the world. Including those scumbags at Black Heir. Why are you putting him at risk now?'

'The Organization could use Black Heir being in our debt, even in an indirect way,' said the Colonel. 'We have to work with these people; but we always work better from a position of strength.'

'How very petty,' said Penny.

'The things that matter most often are,' said the Colonel.

'Who exactly is this old friend of mine?' I said.

'Robert Bergin,' said the Colonel. 'Black Heir referred to him as an information analyst; which probably translates as field agent.'

He looked at me inquiringly, but I just nodded slowly, acknowledging the name.

'I remember him.'

'And is he a friend?' said the Colonel.

'He was, then,' I said. 'But we're talking thirty years ago. People change.'

'Do you want to do him this favour; whatever it is?' said the Colonel. 'You're under no obligation to us to do so.'

'I'll do it,' I said. 'I don't have so many friends that I can afford to turn my back on them.'

The Colonel just nodded. He didn't appear pleased or displeased; this was all just business to him.

'Since this is not an official Organization case, please bear in mind that you won't be able to use our authority or call on any of our resources. Nor should you expect any backup, if things get out of hand.'

'I think I can manage,' I said. 'I did survive a long time on my own, quite successfully, before I joined the Organization.'

'It's a mystery to me how,' said the Colonel.

He handed me a card, with nothing on it but an address in Bradenford, Yorkshire. And then he turned and walked away. Penny and I watched him go, just to make sure he kept going.

'The real question,' I said thoughtfully, 'is how the Colonel knew to find us here . . . I didn't tell anyone we were coming to Soho.'

'And even we didn't know we'd end up here when we started out,' said Penny. 'The Organization must be keeping an eye on you.'

'I'm not sure I approve of that,' I said. 'Especially when I still don't have any real idea of who and what the Organization is. And I really don't like the idea of Black Heir taking a new interest in me.'

'Could the Organization have made some kind of deal?' said Penny. 'To hand you over to Black Heir, in return for something they need?'

'I wouldn't have thought so,' I said. 'Until now.'

'This whole thing could be a trap,' said Penny.

'If it was,' I said, 'I can't help thinking it would have been made to seem more attractive. Even enticing. I haven't a clue what this is all about.'

Penny scowled unhappily. 'What do you remember, about this Robert Bergin?'

'That I owe him.'

Penny waited a while, until she realized that was all I was prepared to say, for the moment.

'What's he like?' she said finally. 'Was he a close friend?'

'A good friend,' I said. 'Back then, I never let anyone get close to me. It wasn't safe; for me,

19

or for them. But we did work a lot of cases together, saved each other's lives more than once, and spent a great deal of time in each other's company. I haven't had any contact with Robert since I walked away from Black Heir in 1988. In something of a hurry, because they were getting a little too curious about my background.'

'You cut him off, just like that?' said Penny. 'That's cold, Ishmael.'

'I was protecting him,' I said flatly. 'From guilt by association. And I never look back. I can't afford to. Because I never know when I'll have to move on again.'

Penny looked like she wanted to say something about that. I waited, to give her the opportunity, but she chose not to.

'And you're ready to help him out, after all these years?' she said. 'Even though it could mean walking into a trap?'

'If he's gone to such lengths to reach out to me, using Black Heir and the Organization, whatever his problem is must be pretty damned important,' I said. 'And I really do owe the man. Still . . . I have to wonder how Robert will react, on seeing me again. It's been thirty years; he must be in his seventies by now. And I'm not.'

'We never talk about this,' Penny said steadily. 'Never talk about the fact that if we stay together, I'll grow older but you won't. Let's say you were born in 1963, when you were first made human. That would make you fifty-five years old, on top of the mid-twenties you appear to be.'

'And I have no way of knowing how many

20

years I lived as my previous self,' I said. 'And whether that was considered young, or old.'

'I can't think about that too much,' said Penny. 'I don't know how to cope with something like that.'

I didn't tell her about the face I'd seen in the mirror that morning, but Penny could tell I was keeping something from her. She always can.

'Does Robert know what you really are?'

'No. He knew there was something different about me; but he never asked and I never told. You're the only person in the world who knows the truth about me. Let's try really hard to keep it that way.'

'So,' Penny said briskly. 'What's our cover going to be, this time?'

'Depends on what the problem is,' I said. 'As far as anyone else needs to know, we're just visiting an old friend.'

'And if it turns out to be more than that?'

I smiled. 'It's always more than that.'

We walked back the way we'd come, arm in arm, like any other young couple out for a stroll on a sunny Saturday morning.

'At least we had a pleasant time together,' said Penny. 'For as long as it lasted. Did you find what you were looking for here?'

'I don't know,' I said. 'I was looking for something from my past, but I don't think it's here any longer. It feels more like something in my past is looking for me.'

'Are we talking about your distant past?' Penny said carefully. 'Your original self?'

21

'I never could keep anything from you.'

I told her about the face in the mirror. The sense that something was stirring in the back of my mind. She just nodded.

'You've been having the bad dreams more often lately. I wish you'd talk about them.'

'I can't,' I said. 'There aren't the words, to describe them.'

'What do you think this thing with the mirror means?'

'I don't know,' I said.

But secretly I wondered if this trip back into my past, into the life of someone I used to be, was such a good idea. Digging up my past was always going to be dangerous for me. And possibly, for everyone around me.

Two
No More Happy Ever Afters

In the end, we took the train to Yorkshire. I like trains. Such a marvellously anonymous way to travel. Penny wasn't keen on driving one of her precious vintage cars all the way up the country to Bradenford, after something tore the engine right out of her precious Rover 25 on our last mission. And besides . . . on this case, even more than usual, I didn't want us doing anything that might attract attention. We didn't have the Organization to run interference for us. It would have been a hell of a long drive, and given that we had no idea of what we were heading into, arriving tired and worn out struck me as a really bad idea. Especially if this plea for help from an old friend did turn out to be some kind of trap, after all.

It was a pretty long journey on the train; hour after hour, station after station. Even the most attractive of scenery can start to grate on the nerves when you've spent half the day rushing past it. Picturesque works best in small doses. Penny had wanted to bring her laptop with her, but I had to say no. You can get tracked far too easily using things like that.

'But I won't go online!' said Penny. 'I'll just use it to watch films!'

'If you don't have it, you can't be tempted to use it,' I said sternly.

Penny sniffed mutinously, but didn't argue. Security was one of the few areas in our life where she was always prepared to defer to me. She looked at me sharply, as a thought struck her.

'Can the Government really tell where we are, using our mobile phones?'

'Not just the Government,' I said.

'Think I'll turn my phone off, for the duration,' said Penny.

I didn't have the heart to tell her that wouldn't make any difference.

So Penny read her *Cosmo* on the train, and dozed a lot. I didn't want to sleep. I was afraid of what I might see in my dreams; or what might see me. I thought hard, turning the problem over and over in my mind. Why was my old self starting to wake up now, after so many years? Could something have been triggered, by my experiences inside the deep dark hole on Brassknocker Hill? Some of the old alien presence had come to the surface once before, when I had to fight the beast at Coronach House, and just a glimpse of it had been enough to scare the hell out of Penny. I'd been able to suppress it, then . . . but I couldn't remember how. I thought long and hard as the train meandered up the long winding spine of the country, but in the end all I had were questions, no answers, and no comfort.

We finally disembarked at the small country town of Bradenford. Just a small rural station in the middle of nowhere, with a few old-fashioned buildings, two platforms, and a few flower displays set out here and there to add a pleasant dash of colour to the otherwise grim surroundings.

Penny and I were the only ones to get off the train at Bradenford, and no one got on before it departed, in something of a hurry. I had to wonder whether it knew something we didn't. Penny and I were left standing alone on the platform, with only two heavy suitcases for company. It was very quiet. The early evening air was pleasantly cool, for this late in the summer, and the light was sharp and clear, as though anxious to show us everything.

'If this was one of your sixties films,' I said finally, 'right about now is when the ominous music would kick in.'

'Let's not throw common sense overboard just yet,' said Penny. 'We're a long way off the beaten track. I'm amazed a town this small still has a station.'

'Robert used to be my friend,' I said. 'Who knows what he is now? We're only here because I owe the man he used to be.'

'This sentimental nature of yours will be the death of you,' said Penny.

'Not if I can help it,' I said. 'Besides; it'll be a nice surprise for him. Always assuming he is who he claims to be.'

'How can you spend your whole life being so paranoid?' said Penny. 'Always thinking around corners, and expecting the worst?'

'Practice.'

Penny headed for the only exit. I picked up

the two suitcases and went after her. We had to pass through the main station building to get to the outside, but the narrow passageway had nothing to offer except shadows and silence. There was no one on duty, and the ticket office was closed. A handwritten sign announced it was only open in the mornings, from 9.00 a.m. to 1.00 p.m.

We emerged from the station to find absolutely nothing waiting for us. No taxis, no bus stop, and not a single vehicle in the small car park. There was no one about and nothing to look at but a single narrow road heading off through open countryside to a small country town some distance away. I dropped the two suitcases. Penny gave me a hard look.

'Tell me you did think to contact your old friend Robert, and inform him we'd be arriving this afternoon?'

'Of course,' I said. 'But all I got was a recorded voice; so I left him a message telling him what time the train would arrive. Circumstances and missed connections permitting.'

We looked at the empty road stretching away before us, without a single vehicle moving on it. They day was warm and pleasant and very quiet.

'Maybe Robert had second thoughts about inviting you here,' said Penny.

'Not after all the trouble he went to, involving Black Heir and the Organization,' I said.

'Then where is he?'

'I don't know!'

'It's not that far,' I said. 'We could always walk.'

'No we couldn't, because yes it really is,' Penny said firmly. 'I did not travel all this way to trudge down a country road carrying two suitcases.'

I thought, but had the good sense not to say out loud, *I don't see why we had to bring this many clothes for such a short stay anyway.* Learning when not to say things like that is at the heart of many a happy relationship. Perhaps fortunately, we were interrupted at that point by the sound of an approaching vehicle. We looked down the road, to where a car was heading our way at considerable speed. Soon enough it skidded to a halt right in front of us, and I looked the car over with mild disbelief. It was probably a pale blue, a long time ago, but now it was old and faded and battered; with a series of scrapes down one side from close encounters with something hard and unyielding. I looked at Penny.

'You're the expert on cars ancient and modern. Is this thing vintage?'

'I think the proper technical term would probably be: a clunker,' Penny said solemnly.

The front door opened with a distinctly aggrieved sound, and the driver got out. He stretched gracefully, and then greeted us with a cheerful smile.

'Hi there! Would you be Ishmael Jones and Penny Belcourt?'

'We would,' I said. 'And you are . . .?'

'Ah! Sorry! I'm David Barnes. Robert sent me to come and get you, because he doesn't drive any more.'

'Why not?' I said.

27

'Too old,' said David.

That thought honestly hadn't occurred to me. I was still thinking of the Robert I used to know; far too many years ago. I gave David my full attention. He appeared to be in his mid-twenties, tall and well-built, with floppy blond hair, a chiselled handsome face and cool blue eyes. He was wearing a tight black leather jacket over a blindingly white shirt, designer jeans and very expensive-looking shoes. He gestured invitingly at the car.

'Climb aboard; and I'll take you straight to see Robert. He's expecting you.'

'Oh good,' said Penny. 'We were beginning to wonder.'

David hurried round to open the back door for Penny, leaving me to take the suitcases round the back. I opened the boot and dumped them in, and by the time I'd finished that Penny was arranging herself in the back seat, and David had slipped behind the steering wheel again. I just had time to open my own door and get in beside Penny, realize there weren't any seatbelts, and then David gunned the engine for all it was worth and went racing off down the long country road to Bradenford.

The road had no markings, but David still somehow contrived to hit every single pothole along the way. Penny and I had to brace our legs against the floor to hold ourselves in place as the car lurched back and forth across the road. David raised his voice, to address us over the strained roar of the engine.

'So! Are you here for the wedding; or the murder?'

Penny and I looked at each other.

'We weren't aware of either of those,' I said carefully.

'Oh,' said David. 'I thought you knew . . . Robert's daughter Gillian is getting married tomorrow, to my best friend, Tom. I'm the best man. Or at least, that was the plan before everything hit the fan.'

Penny let out a long-suffering sigh, and fixed me with a hard look. 'Didn't you just know there'd be a murder?'

'Who's been killed?' I asked David.

He shrugged uncomfortably. 'Ah . . . Robert was really very keen that I wasn't supposed to talk about that. Just get you to him as quickly as possible. And I really don't feel like upsetting him. He can be very stern.'

Penny looked at me. 'Is that the Robert you remember?'

'Pretty much,' I said. 'Is there anything you feel you can talk about, David?'

'Oh sure!' he said. 'I'm an actor! Mostly stage, but a fair bit of television. No movies as yet, but my agent is working on it.'

'Would we have seen you in anything?' Penny said politely.

David brightened up immediately, like any actor with a chance to show off his credits. '*The Wounded Cry*? *Heartless Manoeuvres*? *A Desperate Mourning*? No? Can't say I'm surprised. There's just too many channels these days; and the good stuff gets lost. Heads up! Here comes

Bradenford! A small country town in the middle of nowhere, with far too much past and not enough future, and more character than a bit-part player determined to make an impression.'

We finally entered the town and the road reluctantly improved. There wasn't much traffic about, but the town turned out to be surprisingly pleasant to the eye. The various buildings presented an intriguing mix of architectural styles, covering any number of centuries. Old and new went side by side with no attempt to blend in, or even get along. A well-preserved Norman church stood between a pet shop and a small supermarket, and a long row of Victorian tenements gave way to a series of dull but worthy seventies semi-detacheds. Shops and businesses ranged from old family concerns to modern franchises, to twee little affairs clearly targeted at the tourist trade. The word *Shoppe* appeared frequently, and not in a good way. Penny pointed out an actual thatched cottage, and made excited noises.

'Oh, look at that, Ishmael! Isn't it just divine? I've always wanted to live in one of those!'

'Trust me,' I said. 'You really wouldn't. They're cold, draughty, and the upkeep is crippling.'

'You are not that old,' said Penny.

'I never said I was.'

'It's a lovely town though, isn't it?' said Penny, determined to find a bright side to look on.

'It all seems very nice,' I said. 'But given that we're currently right in the centre of town, doesn't it seem odd to you that there aren't more people about?'

She looked. The streets were almost empty, and the few people out and about appeared to be in something of a hurry. Either because they were on their way to somewhere important, or because they didn't like being out on the streets at this time of the evening.

'It's the country,' David said loudly. 'Probably not much to do here, once it gets dark. They probably roll up the pavements the moment the shops close, to keep the people from wearing them out.'

We passed through the middle of town and just kept going. Soon enough we reached the town outskirts and headed up a narrow lane that headed out into the countryside. David finally brought the old car skidding to a halt before a large and only slightly foreboding detached house, with far too much character for its own good. The nearest neighbours were back at the town, and there was nothing beyond the house but flat open land, stretching off into the distance for as far as the eye could follow, under a cloudless iron-grey sky. The house was a blocky old stone-walled structure, with two stories, diamond-paned windows, and a steeply slanting grey-tiled roof. The general effect was blunt and uncompromising, more like a fortress than a home. And I had to wonder; who or what did my old friend feel the need to defend himself from?

Penny and I got out of the car. It felt good to have solid ground under my feet again, and scenery that wasn't jumping out at me at great speed. I went round to the boot to retrieve the suitcases, while Penny politely thanked David for the lift.

'Sorry I can't stay,' he said quickly. 'But I have to get back to the hotel, and join the bride and groom. I only borrowed this car from the hotel's owner.'

'Aren't you coming in?' said Penny.

'I don't think so,' said David. 'He's really very stern.'

And he turned the car round in a tight arc and sped off back to town. I dropped the suitcases beside Penny.

'He seemed like an amiable sort,' she said.

'He's an actor,' I said.

We stood outside the house with our suitcases, like two refugees or orphans of the storm. There was no one else around, and no reaction from inside the house. It was all very quiet.

'Why aren't there any birds singing?' said Penny, after a while. 'I mean, we're out in the countryside . . .'

'That's moorland,' I said.

'Don't they have birds on the moors?'

I thought about it. 'I don't know.'

We looked around us some more. There was just the one lane, bounded on both sides by open fields, and no one else in sight. No sign of a trap, or an ambush, or any interest in us at all. I looked at the house's front door, and it looked solidly back at me. Penny dug an elbow into my ribs.

'Well?' she said pointedly.

'Well what?'

'Aren't you at least going to ring the bell? Let your old friend know that we've arrived?'

'I'm thinking about it.'

'What's there to think about? Are you worried Robert won't be pleased to see you? He invited you here. Or are you worried that he might be a bit upset, because he got old and you're still young?'

'Those are important things to worry about,' I said, not moving.

'Do you want me to go ring the bell?'

'Not as such . . .'

'Well we can't just stand around here!'

'I'm thinking!' I said.

'Think faster!'

And then we both broke off as the front door opened abruptly, and an old man stared out at us. We stared back at him, and for a long moment no one said anything. The old man might have been tall once, but a stooped back had bent him right over. His hair was grey, what there was of it, and his face was heavily lined, suggesting a lifetime of experience, most of it hard. But his eyes were clear, and his mouth was firm. He was wearing a sleeveless grey cardigan over a plaid shirt, with rough work trousers and brightly-shined black shoes. I didn't recognize him at all. I actually wondered for a moment whether David had brought us to the right house. And then the old man nodded slowly, and addressed me in a voice that was instantly familiar.

'About time you got here, Ishmael. Well, don't stand on ceremony; come on in, the pair of you.'

And just like that I saw something in his face of the man I used to know. Robert Bergin; my old partner in the field, when I worked for Black Heir. Under another name and another identity, all those years ago. I picked up the suitcases and started forward, with Penny sticking close at my side. Robert waited until the last moment to step back out of our way, and invite us into his home with a brusque gesture.

The moment we were all inside, Robert closed the door and locked it. The hall was gloomy and characterless with the outside light cut off. I studied Robert openly. He had to be in his late seventies now, and looked nothing like the dashing field operative I remembered. He looked like his own father, or maybe even grandfather. He didn't spare me or Penny a glance as he headed down the corridor, just growled over his shoulder for me to leave the suitcases in the hall. I placed them carefully to one side, and then Penny and I followed Robert into what turned out to be a perfectly agreeable parlour.

The furniture was generic and well-used, and the carpet's pattern had been all but trodden away, but it all seemed pleasant enough. A few prints of undistinguished landscapes on the walls, and lots of fresh flowers in vases. A presentation clock ticked loudly on the mantelpiece. Evening light streamed in through the window, bathing the room in a friendly glow. It was all very comfortable and cosy. An old man's room. Robert looked at me for a long moment, and I let him. Penny looked quickly from me to him and back again, not sure what to say. Robert studied my face unblinkingly, as though trying

34

to take in every detail, and I couldn't read the expression on his face at all.

'Hello, Robert,' I said finally, because one of us had to start the ball rolling. 'Good to see you again. It's been a while.'

'Thirty years, and change,' said Robert, his voice harsh and dry. 'You haven't changed a bit.' He smiled briefly. 'Unlike me. I'm amazed you can still recognize me. Thanks for coming, Ishmael.'

'Thanks for using my current name,' I said.

'Only polite,' said Robert. 'And it helps to distance me from the man you used to be, all those years ago. But I have to ask; why *Ishmael*?'

'I like it,' I said. 'It's dashing, it's winsome, it's me. I chose it out of thousands. I didn't like the others. They were all too samey.'

Robert shook his head. 'After all these years, you still think you're funny.' He looked at Penny.

'This is my professional partner and the love of my life,' I said. 'Penny Belcourt. She knows all about me, so you can speak openly in front of her. Trust her with anything. I do.'

'Well,' said Robert. 'That's good to know.' He extended a steady hand for her to shake, and her smaller hand disappeared inside his. The handshake was more brisk than polite, but there was a definite twinkle in his eye as he smiled at her. 'Ishmael always did have an eye for a pretty face; and a sense for people he could depend on. I'm glad he's found someone, at last. Sorry to drag you halfway across the country . . . Where are my manners? Sit yourselves down, the pair

35

of you. Would you like some tea? I can put the kettle on . . .'

'We're fine,' I said. 'Let's get down to business.'

'Suit yourself,' said Robert. 'But we've got a lot of talking to do; so sit down and settle yourselves. This is going to take a while.'

He waved us to a heavy sofa with a faded flower pattern, and then lowered himself carefully into the padded and oversized chair facing it. I couldn't take my eyes off him, even as Penny and I sat down. I was stunned by how diminished Robert seemed, compared to the large and powerful man I remembered. The broad shoulders were still there, if somewhat bowed, but the great chest and arm muscles were gone, and there was a definite paunch under the cardigan. The bony hands were speckled with liver spots, and his throat had sunken into a wattle. I realized with a sudden shock that the perfect teeth I saw in his brief smiles were actually dentures. I didn't know why that came as such a shock, but it did.

I had no idea what to say to him. Penny sensed that, and jumped in.

'You have a very nice house, Robert,' she said quickly. 'Quite charming.'

'Don't know as I'd go that far,' said Robert. 'But I like it. Been in the family for generations. Most of what's good about it is down to my wife. Helen always had a gift for nest-building. I never much cared about colours and patterns, fashions and styles and that, but she had enough opinions for both of us. Since she died . . . I

36

don't feel like changing anything. I keep the place tidy, mind. Can't abide a mess. Never could.'

'Of course,' I said. 'You always kept your files arranged so neatly. Every pile of papers carefully squared off on your desk. But I don't remember Helen . . .'

'She was after your time,' said Robert.

'You don't seem all that surprised,' Penny said carefully. 'That Ishmael hasn't aged, like you.'

'He looks exactly the way I remember him,' said Robert, looking me square in the face. 'Not a mark on him, not a day older. Like time stood still, just for him.'

He gestured at a framed photo on an occasional table next to Penny. She picked it up and showed it to me. A man in his forties and a man in his twenties, with eighties' razor-cut hairstyles and Men In Black suits, standing shoulder to shoulder and smiling easily at the camera; ready to take on the world. The younger man was me, the older was Robert.

'I fished that old thing out of the attic the other day,' said Robert, 'Once I decided I needed help. Someone I could depend on.'

Penny offered me the photo. I shook my head, and she put it back on the table.

'I always knew there was something rum about you, Ishmael,' said Robert. 'Never sure what exactly, though I had my suspicions. But I did notice that you never aged a day in all the years we spent together. Which is why I tipped you off, when I realized our superiors at Black Heir were taking an unhealthy interest in your background.'

'Robert understood that I was in danger of becoming the investigated, instead of the investigator,' I said to Penny. 'His warning is what allowed me to make my escape in time, and disappear.'

Penny nodded, understanding at last why I owed this man my time. Robert shrugged briefly.

'Just what friends do for each other. Even if one of them might not be entirely human.'

He raised a bushy grey eyebrow, giving me an opportunity to explain myself. I just smiled, neither confirming nor denying.

'Did you get into any trouble after I left, Robert?'

'No. I was careful to cover my tracks as well as yours. They didn't spend much time looking for you. All they had were a few suspicions, nothing specific enough to alarm them. Far as I know, no one in Black Heir has been interested in you for years.'

'That's good to know,' I said. 'Now; you went to a lot of trouble to reach out to me, Robert. So what's the problem? What is it you need me to do? And why were you so keen that David didn't talk to us about your daughter's wedding, or the murder?'

Robert sat back in his chair, finding the most comfortable position he could for his old bones, and took a moment to consider his words carefully.

'Something is happening here. Something bad. Something . . . out of this world. I don't think it's in my line or yours, Ishmael; and certainly nothing like the cases we used to work. But I'm still hoping you can help me, where the local authorities can't. I'm here on my own, and . . . I'm not the man I used to be. Especially after my wife died, seven years back. You'd have liked her, Ishmael. She wouldn't have taken any nonsense from you either. She worked at Black Heir, in accounting. Our daughter Gillian arrived not long after we were married, and I gave up fieldwork to man a desk. I had responsibilities . . . Now my Gillian is getting married; and she's in danger.

'There was a time I could have protected her myself. You remember what I used to be like, Ishmael. I could take care of myself, and anyone else who needed taking care of. But time is a thief. It takes everything from you, bit by bit, until you're just a shadow of the man you used to be.' He paused to look down at the old hands clasped together in his lap, as though they belonged to someone else. And then he looked back at me. 'But Time hasn't touched you, Ishmael. You look like you can still do what needs doing.'

'Does it bother you?' I said bluntly. 'That I haven't changed?'

'I was relying on it,' said Robert. 'You're everything I need you to be, to protect my daughter from the Bergin family curse.' He paused again, looking carefully at me and Penny, to see if we were prepared to take him seriously. Reassured by what he saw in our faces, he continued.

'It all began back in the eighteenth century, when the Bergin family was a lot more prosperous than it is now. They were rich, powerful, and much looked up to in the area. The eldest daughter was to be married, but the groom had been engaged to someone else. He broke that off, to marry the Bergin daughter. The spurned woman made all kinds of threats, but who was she, to stand against the mighty Bergin family? The marriage went ahead as planned. Half the county was there, to wish the young couple every happiness. But the woman he'd slighted sneaked into the church, and murdered both the bride and the groom, while they were standing at the altar. Stabbed them to death in a frenzy, before the family could drag her away.

'They hanged her, right there in the church, too angry to wait for a trial and official justice.

'But with her last words, the witch put a curse on the Bergin family. That no daughter of theirs would ever be able to marry, because an invisible demon would kill the groom on their wedding night. It would also kill anyone who tried to protect the bride, or get in the way of its vengeance. No more happy ever afters, for a Bergin bride.'

He broke off again, checking to see how we were taking all of this.

'She was a witch?' Penny said finally.

'So they say,' said Robert. 'Though that might have been added to the story later, to explain the curse.'

'I've encountered stranger things,' I said. 'Just how accurate is this story, do you know?'

Robert shrugged. 'It's obviously as much

legend as history. But it's definitely based on an actual event; a real double murder in my family. And quite a few grooms of Bergin brides did die on their wedding nights, in the years that followed. People have written whole books about it, trying to sort out fact from fiction.'

'Those do seem to be quite a few last words, from a woman about to be hanged,' said Penny.

Robert showed us his grim smile again. 'There's no doubt the details have been dramatized down the years, to make for a better story.' The smile vanished as he looked at me sternly. 'But it's not just a story any longer. I believe in this curse, and so should you.'

'What's happened?' I said.

'For many years, the Bergin line produced nothing but sons,' said Robert. 'And the curse became just an old family legend. But now Gillian, my only child, is to be married. And I'm scared for her life, and that of her young man. Scared enough to put you at risk, Ishmael, by reaching out to you through my old contacts at Black Heir. I know the last thing you need is them taking a new interest in you. But there's no one else I can turn to. No one else I can depend on.'

'Take it easy, Robert,' I said. 'I'm here now. Anyone who wants to get to your daughter will have to get through me first. And you should remember, there's damned few that can do that.'

Robert sighed deeply, as though a heavy weight had been lifted off him. 'So you believe in the curse?'

'Let's say, I'm prepared to believe in it. Or

41

something like it. How about your daughter, and her fiancé? Do they believe?'

'No,' said Robert. 'Why should they believe in weird and uncanny things? They don't know the world like we do. Hell, I didn't believe in the curse . . . until the vicar who was to perform the ceremony was found dead, the day before yesterday. Murdered. Left hanging from his own bell rope, in the church where the marriage was to take place. It was only the endless tolling of the bell that made people realize something was wrong. I was one of the people who went to investigate. I was just down the road at the church hall, with my daughter, her fiancé, her bridesmaid and his best man.' He stopped, and looked at me almost apologetically. 'I know, I never used to be religious. But after my Helen died I found a great comfort in the church.'

He waited for me to say something, and when I didn't, he continued. 'The Reverend Allen was a good man. He didn't deserve to die like that, left hanging in his own church just because he agreed to perform the marriage. Despite the legend.'

'He didn't believe in it?' said Penny.

'No,' said Robert. 'People around here mostly do but he said his church, his faith, was a match for any curse. And I laughed, and agreed with him. Now I wonder if I caused his death, by putting him in the firing line.'

'Of course you didn't,' I said flatly. 'We're only responsible for the things we do, not the things other people do. How many times has this curse struck in the past? And when was the last occasion before this?'

42

'I can get you the exact facts and figures if you want,' said Robert. 'But it's got to be a hundred years and more since a Bergin girl tried to marry.'

'And was her husband killed by this invisible demon?' said Penny.

'Torn to pieces on their wedding night,' Robert said levelly. 'The bride went mad from seeing it, and died soon after. No one else saw anything.'

'The vicar being hanged doesn't seem to fit in with that,' I said carefully.

'The church is right in the middle of town,' said Robert. 'With people coming and going all the time. But no one saw anything, or heard anything. Until that damned bell started tolling and wouldn't stop. Like the Devil himself was summoning us, to come and witness his work.'

'What about surveillance cameras in the street outside?' I said

Robert looked at me pityingly. 'This is a small country town. We don't have such things here.'

'And no security measures inside the church?' I said.

'It's a church, Ishmael,' said Robert.

'I have to ask . . .' said Penny. 'Is there any possibility that this could have been a suicide?'

'The police say his neck was broken first, by a heavy blow,' said Robert. 'And then he was strung up afterwards. They're treating it as murder, but we only have a limited police presence here. A single detective, sent over from the next town.' Robert pulled a face. 'I've talked to him. Detective Inspector Peter Godwin. Means well, I suppose. He said they'd send more people when they could, but I don't think I'll hold my breath. We wouldn't have him, if the victim hadn't been a vicar . . . There's no clues, no evidence, no motives. Except perhaps a marriage that an old family curse doesn't want to happen.'

He looked steadily at me and Penny. 'The church where the Reverend Allen died is the same church where the first Bergin bride and groom were murdered, all those years ago. Where the witch put her curse on the family, before she was hanged.'

'And you see a connection,' I said.

'Don't you?' said Robert.

'Who else knew about the curse?' said Penny.

'Everybody!' said Robert. 'It's a well-known story in these parts. I've got some of the better written books about it here in the house, if you want to look at them.'

'Yes,' I said. 'The devil might be in the details.'

'This could just be someone who knows the story,' said Penny, 'and is using it as a smoke-screen to disguise their own purposes.'

'Aye, it could,' said Robert. He looked at me. 'If the problem was straightforward, I wouldn't need you. But this could be complicated in other ways too. Because of who I used to be, and some of the things I did for Black Heir. You can understand that, Ishmael.'

I nodded, but didn't say anything. Because Penny was listening, and there were some things in my past I wasn't ready to share with her.

'When is the wedding supposed to take place?' said Penny.

'Tomorrow,' said Robert. 'And Gillian is

determined to go ahead. The guests are all on their way, and we're getting another vicar from two towns over. He doesn't believe in the curse either.'

'You're not giving me much time to do anything,' I said.

'I tried to convince Gillian to postpone the wedding,' said Robert. 'But she's stubborn. Takes after her mother.'

'And her father,' I said.

'Aye. Maybe,' said Robert.

'What do you want me to do?' I said. 'What do you think I can do?'

'You were always a first-class field agent,' Robert said steadily. 'And a damn sight more open-minded than most of the people we worked with at Black Heir. If it wasn't alien in origin, they didn't know what to do with themselves. I need you to find out what's happening and put a stop to it. Whether it's a curse, a murderer hiding behind an old story; or something from our shared past come back to haunt me.'

'You think it might be?' I said.

'I retired from Black Heir twenty years ago,' said Robert. 'I can't think of any old enemies, or unfinished cases, that might still pose a threat . . . But a lot of the things you and I did back in the day had consequences.' He looked down at his wrinkled hands, clenched into fists. An impotent gesture, and he knew it. 'I can't protect my own daughter. So I had no choice but to send for a man who could.'

I nodded. 'You need to understand, Robert. If I go looking for the truth, then that's what I'll find. No matter how far I have to go, or who it hurts. Are you sure that's what you want?'

'Whatever it takes,' said Robert. 'Just . . . save my daughter.'

'And the man she's marrying,' said Penny.

'Oh aye, him as well,' said Robert. 'Tom; he's a good lad. An actor, but I don't hold that against him. We all have to make a living. Aye . . . A good man for my daughter.' He smiled quickly. 'Or this marriage wouldn't be taking place anyway.'

'Then I'm on the case,' I said.

'Me too!' said Penny.

'Of course,' I said. 'I couldn't do it without you.'

'And don't you forget it,' said Penny.

I looked at Robert. 'What are you smiling at?'

Three
Loose Ends from the Past

Robert looked at the clock on the mantelpiece, took in the time, and rose stiffly to his feet. He made a series of harsh noises without realizing, just from the effort of stirring his old bones into movement. I thought again of the powerful and athletic man he used to be. It didn't seem that long ago. I got to my feet, and Penny got to hers.

'You're welcome to stay here,' said Robert. 'There's a spare room that hardly ever gets used.'

'That would be fine,' I said.

I hadn't looked for a hotel in town, because I hadn't been sure whether I'd want to take the case. And of course if it had been a trap, my captors would have supplied the room.

Robert led the way out into the hall, and started up the stairs. He made more noises, as he took his time climbing them. Penny gestured at the suitcases further down the hall, and I went back to get them as she started after him. By the time I'd retrieved the suitcases and caught up with them, they were still only halfway up.

The stairs were narrow wooden steps with no carpeting, all of which protested loudly under our weight. That's an old agent's trick, to make sure you always know when someone is coming. There were no prints or decorations on the wall, just flower-patterned wallpaper. Someone in this house really loved flowers, and I doubted it was Robert. Everywhere he went in the house it must have felt like being haunted by reminders of his dead wife. Presumably he found that comforting.

Robert stopped at the top of the stairs to get his breath, and Penny and I waited patiently until he was ready to lead us down the landing to the room at the far end. He pushed open the door to reveal a space so small you couldn't even manage a decent wind up to swing a cat. Robert waited for me to nod approval, like a waiter presenting a bottle of wine he wasn't sure about, and then led the way in. There was nothing in the room apart from a bed and a chest of drawers, with so little room between them and the wall that we had to enter in single file. The window was wide open, to let in some fresh air. I put the suitcases on the bed. There was nowhere else to put them.

'I made the bed up this morning, just in case you were coming,' said Robert. 'The room hasn't been used in a while.'

I didn't need him to tell me that. My more than human sense of smell wasn't picking up any human traces, just lots and lots of dust. I didn't say that out loud. I'd always been careful not to reveal any of my extra abilities to Robert. He might have been my partner, but he was still Black Heir.

'Bathroom is on the other side of the landing,' Robert said gruffly. 'The door opposite. All the

48

hot water you want, but be careful when you flush the toilet. It doesn't like surprises.'

'Your daughter isn't staying here with you?' said Penny.

'No,' said Robert. He didn't sound disappointed, but he must have seen a question in my expression. 'Gillian's at the hotel, in town. Said she didn't want to be any trouble. I wouldn't have minded; I would have been glad of the company. But . . . Gillian and her mother were always having words. Put two strong-minded women together under the same roof, and they'll always find something to disagree over. They made up as fast as they fell out; but not the last time, just before Helen died. I think being in this house again brought back more bad memories than good, for Gillian. So she and her Tom took a room at The Swan.'

'Just the one room?' Penny said innocently.

Robert surprised me then, with another of his brief smiles. 'I didn't mind, though Gillian probably thought I should. Just so she could tell me to mind my own business. Young people always think they invented sex. The best man and the bridesmaid have rooms there too.'

'We'll go and have a word with them, once we've unpacked,' I said.

Robert looked a little taken aback. 'No need to rush off. I thought we could talk first, about old times . . .'

'We don't have the time,' I said flatly. 'Your daughter is getting married tomorrow, at . . .?'

'Two p.m.,' said Robert.

'Then the clock is ticking, and we're under the

49

gun,' I said. 'We need to get started straight away. There'll be time for reminiscences when this is all over.'

Robert nodded stiffly. 'Of course. I don't drive any more, so I'll have to call for a taxi to take you back into town.'

He left the room and stomped off down the landing. Penny and I looked round the room. It didn't take long. Penny waited till she was sure Robert was out of earshot, and then fixed me with a hard look.

'We travelled all this way, just to sleep in an over-sized cupboard? That's a single bed, Ishmael! And there is such a thing as too much togetherness.'

'I've lived in smaller places than this,' I said, just to be contrary. 'I like a room where you can lie on the bed and put your hand on anything just by reaching out.'

'Down boy,' Penny said dryly. 'Business first, pleasure later.' She shook her head slowly. 'A family curse, Ishmael? Really? In this day and age? What did you make of that story?'

I shrugged. 'We've worked stranger cases. And England is famous for its ghosts and revenants. Echoes of events that won't stay quiet. Loose ends from the past, still haunting the present.'

'Speaking of which,' said Penny. 'Robert said he was worried that some of the things he did for Black Heir might be coming back to haunt him. What kind of things is he talking about, Ishmael? Were you involved in any of them?'

I sat down on the bed, and gestured for Penny to sit next to me. She did so, and I lowered my

50

voice; even though I could tell there was no one else nearby. Some learned cautions can't be unlearned.

'Black Heir isn't like the Organization, Penny. They don't investigate mysteries, solve problems, or help people in trouble. Their sole remit is to tidy up after close encounters. Repair any damage, remove any bodies, make sure there's no evidence left and salvage any useful tech.'

Penny couldn't keep the grin off her face. 'You really were Men In Black!'

'Trust me,' I said. 'It was nothing like the films. And sometimes we had to deal with what was left of the people who'd been involved in these situations.'

Penny stopped smiling. She lowered her voice too, as though she didn't want anyone to hear what she was saying. And perhaps because she wasn't sure she was going to approve of what I might say in response.

'Did you threaten these people? Intimidate them into not talking? Ishmael, are you saying you . . .?'

'We talked to them,' I said. 'Showed them faked evidence, to persuade them they hadn't seen what they thought they saw. If that didn't work, standard operating procedure was to encourage them with wild theories, and then put them in touch with the more extreme alien contact groups. So nothing they said would ever be taken seriously.'

'That sounds a bit cruel,' said Penny.

'It was for their own protection,' I said. 'And everyone else's. Humanity is better off not knowing about some of the things they share this planet with. But all we ever did was talk. We never raised a hand to anybody.'

'Then what is Robert so worried about?' said Penny.

I chose my words carefully. 'No Black Heir field agent ever had direct contact with aliens. I never even saw one from a distance.'

'Did you want to?'

'I thought about it a lot, but . . . in the end I decided I was better off not pushing my luck. I couldn't risk coming into contact with something that might wake my other self. And besides that . . . People who did have direct contact with aliens often ended up damaged. Physically and mentally. There were chemical spills, radiations we didn't even have names for, and sometimes . . .'

'What did you do with those people?' said Penny. 'The damaged ones?'

'The Government maintains a special hospital and secret holding centre on the Isle of Wight,' I said. 'Where people can be kept in strict isolation. It's called the Hazard Asylum.'

'And these people stay there, until they're well enough to go home?'

'I don't think anyone's ever gone home,' I said. 'Because we don't know how to repair the physical and mental damage caused by things not of this Earth. All we can do is care for them, as best we can, for as long as we can.'

Penny looked at me. 'Is it . . . a bad place?'

'I don't know,' I said. 'I was never sent there, and all files concerning the Asylum were heavily restricted. I heard stories, but there are always stories.' I stopped for a moment, to make sure my voice was steady before I continued. 'I used to have nightmares. All the time I was working for Black Heir. That one day I would be ordered to escort someone to the Asylum; and once I was inside they'd say "We know what you are". And I'd never get to go home again.'

I had to stop. Penny held my hand, giving me time to collect myself.

'Robert was always the one who decided which people could be helped, and which needed to be sent away,' I said finally. 'He knew I couldn't do that.'

Penny looked at me for a long moment, too shocked to speak. 'That nice old man decided who got locked up for life?' she said finally. 'Just because they were in the wrong place at the wrong time?'

'It had to be done!' I said sharply. 'They were too damaged to survive on their own, and too dangerous to other people to be allowed to run loose. The Asylum could keep them alive; and keep them from hurting anyone else.'

'I'm not sure I understand,' said Penny. 'What do you mean, when you say damaged?'

'Most of the aliens who come here are nothing like the things you see in films and on television,' I said. 'They're not cute like ET, or on *Star Trek* where they're just people with pointed ears and bumps on their noses. Most aliens are so different from what we think of as life, that any kind of contact is actually toxic. I'm talking about the kind of damage where dying would

53

be kinder. Why do you think I have so many nightmares about what I used to be, before I was made human? Why I'm so scared of what I might do if it ever wakes up, and gets out?'

'And Robert sent these people to the Asylum,' said Penny. 'Have any of them ever escaped?'

'Not as far as I know. But if one of them got out, and has come here looking for revenge . . .'

Penny didn't look at me. She had a lot to think about.

'Are there many of these close encounters to clean up after?' she said finally.

'More than you'd think,' I said. 'That's why the Government needs a whole department just to stay on top of them.'

'How long has this been going on for?'

'I don't think anyone knows for sure.'

'But . . . Why do all these aliens keep coming here?' said Penny.

'A lot of people would like to know the answer to that one,' I said. 'I believe there's a war going on. Out there. And we're just caught in the middle, like one of those small islands in the Pacific back in the Second World War. Where the opposing armies came and went, fighting their battles, and the native islanders never did understand what it was all about.'

Penny shuddered suddenly. 'That's scary.'

'Yes,' I said. 'It is.'

I left Penny to unpack the suitcases, while I went across the landing and into the bathroom. She needed some time alone, to think; and I didn't want to talk any more. I'd worked hard to have a human life, while doing my best to protect Humanity from monsters like me. I looked into the mirror over the bathroom sink. I looked tired, drawn, haunted. My face might still be young, but my eyes were old. I ran some cold water into the sink, and splashed it across my face. It wasn't as refreshing as I'd hoped, but it made me feel like I was doing something. When I raised my head to look back into the mirror, my other self was there.

I froze. I wanted to scream, but I couldn't. My original self was back, and there was nothing I could do to make it go away. The mirror grew larger, expanding in all directions as my other self pressed forward, trying to force its way through. It grew bigger and bigger, looming over me. Every nightmare I'd ever had, only real. Horror in the flesh, awful beyond bearing. My inner demon, from some alien hell. It was trying to say something to me but I couldn't understand. I didn't want to understand. I squeezed my eyes shut and refused to believe what was happening. Fighting it with all my will.

When I could finally bear to open my eyes again, the mirror was back to normal. There was nothing in the reflection but my human face, bone white and dripping with sweat. My eyes were wide, and my mouth was trembling. My whole body was shaking so badly I had to put both hands on the sink to support myself. Why was my old self rising up now, out of the depths of my mind? What was it trying to tell me? That my time was over, and I needed to step aside? I straightened up, shaking my head. Never. I had worked so hard to be human. It was all I'd ever been, and all I ever wanted to be. I wouldn't give it up. I would live as a man, and if need be die as a man; to keep the beast from breaking out of its cage.

Penny's voice came to me from across the landing, from another life.

'Ishmael? Is everything all right?'

I reached for the towel to dry my face, and when I answered Penny my voice was perfectly calm and normal.

'I'm fine. Everything's fine. I'll be with you in a moment.'

Not long after, I went downstairs with Penny. She could tell something was wrong, but since I was refusing to talk about it, she couldn't either. What could I say to her? That I was damaged; and should have been sent to the Hazard Asylum?

'Let's just concentrate on the job at hand,' I said, staring straight ahead. I've always found it easier to lie to Penny when I don't have to look her in the eye. 'We need to find whoever killed the vicar before they can get to Robert's daughter. That's all that matters.'

'Of course,' said Penny. 'We can do that.'

When we got to the foot of the stairs Robert was there waiting for us. He offered me two paperback books, both about the Bergin curse. I took them from him and studied the covers. The more garish of the two showed a huge mansion house at night, surrounded by shadows, with a light blazing from one window. A pretty young woman in a frilly nightdress was running from the house. The book was called, *The Bergin Curse.* The tagline: *What terrible secret was revealed on her wedding night?* The other book at least tried for a more sober approach. The cover showed a series of tombstones, all bearing the Bergin name. The title was: *A Bloodline of Murder.* The tagline: *The facts behind the Bergin legend.*

'These two cover the basics best, in their own ways,' said Robert.

I stuffed the books into my jacket pockets, for later. 'They look interesting.'

'I'm sure they'll be very useful,' Penny said kindly. 'Thank you, Robert.'

'There's a taxi waiting outside, to take you into town,' said Robert. 'I've phoned ahead to The Swan to tell Gillian you're on your way. I told her you're here to help, and that she can trust you.'

'We'll be back later this evening,' I said. 'Hopefully we'll have more to talk about then.'

Penny and I went outside, and the first thing I noticed was that it was getting dark. A cheerful voice addressed us from the waiting taxi. The driver was a large woman in an Atomic Blonde T-shirt and a battered black leather jacket. She had a broad happy face and a mop of straw-yellow curls that looked thick enough to break any comb that came near it.

'Hello, Ishmael, hello Penny! I'm Cathy! Hop in; Mr Bergin's told me all about you!'

'I doubt that,' I said.

Penny elbowed me in the ribs. I looked back

at the front door, but Robert had already closed it. I headed for the taxi, with Penny sticking close beside me.

'This should be interesting,' she said.

'I hate interesting,' I growled.

'Climb aboard for the mystery tour!' Cathy said grandly. 'The real mystery being how we can provide such excellent service at such reasonable prices. Come on, shake a leg! I don't bite! Not on a first date, anyway.'

I looked at Penny. 'I think I preferred the other ride.'

'Play nicely, Ishmael,' said Penny, smiling determinedly. 'It's a long walk into town. And don't say anything to upset the driver. She looks like she could crush both of us with one thumb.'

We climbed into the back of the taxi. The seats were comfortable, and there were seatbelts. Cathy actually waited until we were settled before turning the taxi around in a tight arc and heading back to town. The last of the light was dropping out of the day, and the first traces of mist appeared in the taxi's headlights. The lights from the town glowed in the distance, like beacons in the night. Cathy had already pushed the glass partition back, so she could chat cheerfully to us over her shoulder.

'So! You know Mr Bergin! Good for you. Everyone around here knows Mr Bergin. His family goes way back. The local churchyard is so full of his ancestors we're having to bury new bodies on top of each other, just to fit them in. Mr Bergin's dad went to school with my dad, and I went to school with his daughter.'

'You and Gillian are friends?' said Penny.

'On and off,' said Cathy. 'She was always one of the cool kids, while I settled for being popular. Or easy, if you prefer. So, are you guys here for the wedding? Or the murder?'

'We're wedding guests,' I said. 'Though of course we are interested in the murder. What have you heard?'

'Just the essentials,' said Cathy. 'The vicar got his neck stretched in church, like the old witch, and now the whole town's panicking. Thinking the curse has come back to get them. Everyone's got their own take on what happened, but no one knows anything. Except that the murderer is still out there, somewhere.'

'Is that why there's hardly anyone about?' said Penny.

'Of course! What do you expect?' said Cathy. 'The killer could be anyone! Everyone with any sense is staying inside, barricading their doors and nailing their windows shut.'

'But you're not scared?' I said.

Cathy laughed heartily. 'Anyone even looks at me sideways, I'll kick him so hard in the nuts they'll end up in different counties. Everyone around here knows better than to mess with me.'

'Did you know the vicar?' I said.

'Not really,' said Cathy. 'I'm not religious. Except for christenings, weddings and funerals. And Christmas carol services. I do like a good carol. But otherwise, I don't have the time. I knew the Reverend Allen to speak to, because it's a small town. You can't walk round the supermarket without bumping into a dozen

59

people you'd rather avoid. Everyone knows everyone in a town like this, if you get my drift. Not so much a gene pool as a gene puddle. Half the kids in school have the same big ears. And more than a few have the same father, despite who their mothers married. We're going to have to do something about George. Probably involving a sharp blade or two bricks banged together.'

'About the Reverend Allen . . .' said Penny.

'Oh, he was all right,' said Cathy. 'For a vicar. Never preached outside the church, and never tried to shove anything down your throat.' She caught my eye in the rear-view mirror, and dropped me a roguish wink. 'Not that I would have minded. He looked like he might have been fun, if he could just bring himself to let someone else's hair down.'

I waited for her to draw a breath so I could butt in with a question. 'Do you believe in the Bergin curse?'

'Are you kidding?' said Cathy. 'That stuff is strictly for the tourists. Though everyone in town is talking about it now.'

'Are there any strangers in town?' said Penny.

'Not really,' said Cathy. 'Tourist season is pretty much over. They come and go with the summer. We're not on the way to anywhere, so no one's ever just passing through. Not this far out on the moor. Once it gets to September, we're mostly just selling stuff to each other so we can survive until summer comes round again. The only new faces right now are people like your-selves, here for the wedding.'

'Who do you think killed the vicar?' said Penny.

'Beats the hell out of me,' Cathy said cheerfully. 'Haven't a clue. Just like the police, from what I'm hearing. Could be anybody. Which is pretty damned creepy if you think about it. Still, you do hear things these days, about vicars, priests . . . Not that I ever heard anything like that about the Reverend Allen, and in a town this size you'd be bound to. He seemed nice enough; but then, they always do, don't they? Killers? You never know who anyone is really, on the inside.'

'Everyone has their secrets,' I said. 'Some more than others.'

'Not me!' Cathy said happily. 'My whole life is an open book, with all the dirty pages clearly marked. Not to mention very well-thumbed, if I say so myself.'

'Oh look!' said Penny, with a certain sense of relief. 'Isn't that The Swan, right ahead?'

'Well spotted!' said Cathy.

She pulled up outside the hotel, right in front of the main entrance. Ignoring the double yellow lines and the prominent *No Parking* sign. She turned round in her seat, to grin at me and Penny. Rather like a friendly ogre who'd decided not to eat us after all.

'Look, I know everyone and everything that goes on in this town. You need anything, here's my card. No, wait a minute, that's my domination services . . . This card. Call me any time.'

Penny took the card, and then looked at me meaningfully.

'I paid for the last taxi.'

'So you did,' I said.

I passed Cathy the fare, including a tip nicely calculated to appear grateful but not generous. I wasn't sure I wanted to encourage Cathy. She didn't even look at the money, just dropped it into a box beside her seat. Penny and I got out of the taxi, and Cathy fixed me with a grin.

'Have a good time at the wedding; and try not to get murdered!'

The taxi disappeared off down the road, and it was suddenly very quiet outside the hotel. It took me a moment to come up with just the right comment.

'She was a real . . .'

'Character,' Penny said quickly.

'Yes,' I said. 'I'm almost certain that was the word I was looking for.'

We gave The Swan our full attention. Set between a solicitor's and a florist's, neither of which seemed to be particularly flourishing, The Swan appeared positively Elizabethan. Old grey stone, half-timbered frontage, with latticed windows and three jutting gables. The whole building had a squat, solid air, as though it had been there for a long time and had no intention of going anywhere. It didn't look particularly welcoming, but it did seem solid and secure enough to offer a safe haven from the night.

Once we were inside, the cosy little lobby turned out to be surprisingly modern, with gleaming well-polished wooden surfaces and a parquet floor. The reception desk boasted its own

62

computer, a helpful sign about Wi-Fi, and a whole bunch of tourist brochures. Sitting behind the desk was a middle-aged lady with a bony face, a fixed smile, and a rather obvious blonde wig. She studied Penny and me unblinkingly, like a wolf that had just spotted fresh prey. But before she could say anything a young man and woman hurried forward to greet us.

Gillian Bergin introduced herself first, in a brisk no-nonsense way. She thrust out a hand for a firm handshake, and then looked us over critically. Gillian was tall and well-built, a good-looking brunette in her late twenties, suggesting she'd been a late child for Robert. She was wearing a smart blue pinstripe suit, and sensible shoes. Her hair was short but stylish, her smile came and went, and she had the look of a woman who knew her own mind. And didn't have much patience for those who couldn't keep up with her.

Tom Stone introduced himself in a calm languid way, as though to apologize for his fiancé's manner. He was almost as tall as Gillian, good-looking in a practiced and rather louche way, and effortlessly charming. He was in his late twenties too, with an athlete's figure, jet-black hair and a handshake he'd clearly practiced to make it as sincere and brief as possible. He was wearing a vintage Black Sabbath T-shirt under a cream jacket, with designer Levis and trainers. He gave us his name with enough emphasis to suggest we were supposed to recognize it.

'Of course,' I said. 'Robert told us you were an actor.'

63

'He's very talented,' said Gillian. 'And he's going to be big. If I have anything to say about it.'

'No one can stand against Gillian when she puts her mind to something,' said Tom. 'She's like a force of nature. Aren't you, darling?'

'There's a bar here, where we can talk privately,' Gillian said briskly. She shot a quick look at the receptionist, who was clearly drinking in every word. 'That's Nettie. She owns this place, though she has to do most of the work herself. Not a bad sort, but it's hard to have a conversation anywhere in the hotel without looking up to find her hovering in the background.'

'Wouldn't surprise me if she bugged the rooms,' said Tom. 'Just to make sure no one's getting up to anything they shouldn't.' He smiled at Gillian. 'Though you know I always perform best in front of a camera.'

A brief snort of laughter forced its way past Gillian's composure. 'Stop it, Tom.'

'Certainly, darling. Which way did it go?'

Gillian led us into the adjoining bar. She didn't glance back once to make sure we were following, as though it honestly never occurred to her that we wouldn't. The bar, which was hardly any larger than the lobby, turned out to be deserted. Which was somewhat surprising, at this time of the evening. The illumination was cheerful without being too bright, the tables were clean and the chairs looked comfortable enough. And best of all, no piped music. It all seemed pleasant enough. So where was everyone?

'There's hardly anyone staying in the hotel,'

said Gillian, answering the question I hadn't asked. 'Off season, I suppose. I've hardly run into anyone in the corridors, or the restaurant. The food here's passable, by the way. If you're not too fussy.'

'Nettie is positive the vicar's death will pull in the tourists,' said Tom. 'People do love a good murder; from a safe distance.'

'You should know,' said Gillian. 'You've appeared in enough detective shows.'

'Sometimes the detective, sometimes the murderer,' said Tom. 'I'm adaptable.'

The bartender turned out to be a surly teenager, dressed in a formal outfit that would have made him look quite presentable, if he hadn't been slouching so defiantly. He had a face full of acne and no character, and radiated the standard teenage air of: *this is all a waste of my time.* He pretended to be immersed in his copy of *Kerrang!* magazine as we lined up at the bar. Tom murmured that this was Albert, Nettie's son. I rapped on the wooden bar with a knuckle, loud enough to make Albert jump. He started to glare at me, took a good look and thought better of it. He dropped his magazine and straightened up.

'Is there anything I can do for you, sir?' he said. In a way that suggested he very much doubted it.

'I'm in the chair!' Tom said cheerfully. 'What's everyone having?'

Gillian had a glass of house red, Tom had a G&T, Penny had her usual Campari and soda, and I had a brandy. Alcohol doesn't actually do anything for me, but I learned long ago that people tend to relax more if they think I'm drinking too. Albert busied himself with the drinks as the quickest way of getting rid of us, and we then moved to a table on the other side of the bar. I'd been quietly studying Gillian and Tom's body language. They seemed easy enough in each other's company, but Gillian was clearly the dominant partner. In public, at least. And yet . . . I couldn't help thinking they both seemed a little too relaxed, for people under a death sentence from a family curse.

'Where are the best man and bridesmaid?' said Penny, after we'd all tried our drinks. 'Will they be joining us?'

'They've locked themselves in their rooms,' said Gillian. 'Though they've promised to come out in time for the wedding. David Barnes is Tom's oldest friend, and I've known Karen Nicholls since we started working together.'

'They were both badly affected by the vicar's death,' said Tom.

'And you're not?' I said.

'It was a shock,' said Gillian, meeting my gaze steadily. 'But I don't let things get to me.'

'I can always rely on Gillian to be strong enough for both of us,' said Tom, taking a good swig of his drink. 'But I have to say, I'm surprised how many people around here seem to be taking this whole curse thing very seriously.'

'People have been queuing up all day to take a look at the murder scene,' said Gillian. 'Ghoulish, I call it.'

'They all disappeared a bit sharpish, once it started getting dark,' said Tom.

'Has the vicar's unusual manner of death attracted much attention from the media?' I said.

'Not from any of the national papers,' said Tom. 'Or any of the television companies. Apparently one dead vicar isn't a big enough story, these days. Of course, the local paper is all over it, but that's just one girl reporter and her cameraman.'

Gillian snorted loudly. 'She's loving all this. Interviewing anyone who'll stand still long enough, and getting photographs of anything that doesn't run away. She thinks she can make a career out of this story if she plays her cards right, and move up in the world.' She looked at me thoughtfully. 'You can bet she'll fasten on to you soon enough, once she realizes you're investigating the murder.'

I didn't like the idea of media attention. Or anything that might make it harder for me to stay safely under the radar, now I didn't have the Organization's usual protections. While I was thinking about that, Penny moved quickly in to fill the pause.

'Robert asked us to work out what's really going on,' she said. 'See if we can get to the bottom of things. And make sure the two of you get married safely, of course.'

'Why you two?' Gillian said bluntly. 'Dad went out of his way to assure me that we could trust you, but he didn't say why. What's so special about you?'

'Yes,' said Tom. 'Do tell.'

'Robert and I used to work together,' I said. 'Some time ago.'

'Really?' Gillian was suddenly much more interested in me. 'Dad would never tell me who he used to work for, except that it was something to do with security and I couldn't talk about it to anyone. But of course I did. Made me top girl in the playground for years. Are you . . .?'

'Sorry,' I said. 'That's classified.'

'You don't know what I was about to ask!'

'Whatever it was, it's classified,' I said calmly.

That actually seemed to reassure her. She liked the idea that I was a professional of some kind, and someone who could be taken seriously.

'But you're not police?' said Tom.

'Not as such,' said Penny, happy to muddy the waters some more. 'We're just helping out.'

Tom studied my face thoughtfully. 'You don't look old enough to have worked with Robert before he retired. Have you had work done?'

Gillian slapped his arm, a little too hard to be playful. 'Tom! That's such an actory thing to say!'

Tom smiled and shrugged, apparently not bothered by the slap. Maybe he was used to it.

'It's in the genes,' I said smoothly. 'I can't take any credit.'

Penny looked like she wanted to slap my arm, but settled for smiling determinedly at Tom. 'We don't normally get to meet real actors. Have you been in anything we might have seen recently?'

Tom brightened up immediately, another actor eager to give us his credits. '*The Deaf Detective*?

68

Murder On The Quiet? Death Comes Knocking? No? I was on *Coronation Street* for several weeks, as a travelling salesman with a secret . . .'

Penny recognized some of that. I didn't. Tom looked quietly resigned, and addressed himself to his drink.

'Never mind, darling,' said Gillian. 'You can show them your reviews later.' She turned back to me. 'Has Dad been talking to you about that stupid curse?'

'You don't believe in it?' I said.

'Of course not!' said Gillian. 'It's just superstitious nonsense!'

'I don't know,' said Tom. 'People around here seem to be taking it all extremely seriously . . .'

Gillian looked at him, and he stopped talking.

'So you don't think the Reverend Allen's death was in any way connected to your wedding?' said Penny.

'No,' said Gillian, very firmly. 'It's just a horrible coincidence. And it's not going to stop us getting married tomorrow! Right, Tom?'

'Of course,' Tom said quickly. 'Absolutely.' He looked at me steadily. 'Gillian's had her heart set on getting married in her old church, in her old town, with her father leading her down the aisle. And if that's what Gillian wants, I am ready to do whatever it takes to make sure she gets it.'

Gillian patted his arm approvingly, and they shared a fond smile.

'What did you make of the Reverend Allen?' I said.

'We only met him a few times,' said Gillian. 'He's new. Only been in the town a few years.'

'Long enough to make enemies?' I said.

'No one's said anything . . .' said Gillian. She looked at Tom, who shrugged. She looked back at me. 'He seemed pleasant enough. But then, that's part of a vicar's job, isn't it?'

'I thought he seemed pleasant,' said Tom.

He'd finished his drink, and was glancing restlessly at Gillian and the bar. Apparently he wasn't allowed to order another drink until Gillian had finished hers. And she was too busy fixing me with her best hard stare.

'What can you do to help, that the regular police can't?'

'We can ask questions,' I said. 'People will often talk to us when they wouldn't open up to the authorities. And there's always the chance we might spot something the police have missed.'

'We're very good at that,' said Penny.

Gillian didn't seem particularly convinced, but she didn't want to argue.

'I'm just relieved someone's turned up to help,' said Tom, jumping valiantly into the pause. 'I might play a detective on television now and again, but I wouldn't have a clue what to do in real life.' He smiled at Gillian. 'All I can do is look after you. Stand between you and all harm.'

'Of course you will,' said Gillian. 'Just like you know I'd never let anything happen to you.'

She took his hand in hers, and for a moment they only had eyes for each other.

I cleared my throat, to get their attention back again. 'Robert said there was a policeman in town. What's he like?'

Tom sniffed loudly. 'Detective Inspector Godwin; straight out of central casting. Young and keen and so far out of his depth scuba gear wouldn't save him. The one they only send out when everyone else is busy.'

'He was very rude to us!' said Gillian, her eyes flashing at the memory. 'Practically accused us of withholding information, just because we didn't want to talk about the stupid curse!'

'You told him, darling,' said Tom.

'Damn right I did,' said Gillian. She gave me another of her hard looks. 'Are you going to talk to him?'

'Not if I can help it,' I said.

Tom leaned forward across the table, suddenly serious. 'Can you keep Gillian safe? I mean, I'm not worried about the curse, obviously. And I won't leave her side for a moment until we're safely married. But there is a murderer out there, somewhere. I had to lock the door and jam a chair up against it last night, before Gillian could get to sleep.'

'He's very protective,' said Gillian, shooting Tom another fond look. 'Even though he knows I can look after myself. Do you think we'll be safe, once we're married?'

'If this murder is connected to the curse,' I said carefully. 'But there's always the chance someone is using the curse as a smokescreen, to hide their true motives. The vicar's death could be connected to you, or your father's old job, or as you said earlier, it could just be a horrible coincidence. The only sure way for you to be entirely safe, is for us to uncover the murderer.'

'And we're really very good at that,' said Penny.

'The two of you were in the church hall, when the vicar was murdered,' I said.

'That's right,' said Gillian. 'It was a wedding rehearsal. Tom and me, David and Karen, and Dad. We were waiting for the Reverend Allen to join us, so we could discuss some changes to our vows. We didn't know anything had happened, until that awful bell started ringing and Dad went to see what was up.'

Tom shuddered, just a bit theatrically. 'I hate to think that while we were arguing over a few words, that poor man was dying . . .'

'It wasn't just a few words,' Gillian said sharply. 'It was our wedding vows! These things matter!'

'Of course, darling,' Tom said quickly. 'This is your dream wedding. Every detail is important.'

I decided this would be a good time to leave. I gave the nod to Penny, and we both got to our feet. Gillian and Tom looked at us in surprise.

'You're going?' said Gillian.

'Stay and have another drink!' said Tom.

'There are things we need to do,' I said. 'We can talk more later. I think Penny and I need to visit the church. Take in the murder scene, get a feel for the place and a sense of what happened.'

'It was very nice to meet both of you,' said Penny.

We left the bar quickly, while Gillian and Tom launched into what sounded like an ongoing discussion about flower arrangements, and who would be sitting next to whom at the reception afterwards.

As we walked through the lobby, the receptionist hailed us in a high reedy voice. We stopped, and turned to look at her.

'Hello, dears! I'm Nettie, and this is my little domain. Can I just ask; will you be staying with us?'

'We're guests for the Bergin wedding,' I said. 'And we're staying with Robert Bergin.'

'Oh, that's nice,' said Nettie. 'He could use some company. He's been all alone since Helen died, the poor thing.'

'Do you know about the family curse?' said Penny.

'Oh yes, dear,' said Nettie, quite offhandedly. 'Everyone around here knows about that. Our one claim to fame.'

'Does everyone believe in it?' I said.

'Of course, dear!' said Nettie. 'We're all brought up to take every word as gospel.' She glanced across at the bar. 'And those poor dears, so determined to go ahead with their wedding, despite everything. So brave . . . I don't know where we're going to find space in the church-yard to bury them . . .'

'Did you know the vicar?' I said.

'The Reverend Allen? Of course, dear. Lovely man. Very keen. I don't go to church myself, you understand, but I'd often see him in the town and he always had a kind word for me. It's so sad, what's happened. I keep hoping someone will come along and tell us it was all just a horrible accident.'

'So he didn't have any enemies?' said Penny.

'No, dear!' said Nettie. 'I'd have heard.'

'Can you give us directions to the church?' I said.

Nettie straightened up, to give me her best shocked look. 'You don't want to be going there, dear! Not now, not at this time of night.'

'We'll be fine,' I said. 'We're not scared of the dark.'

'No one ever is, dear,' said Nettie. 'Until something comes out of the dark to get them.'

She provided us with directions. They were easy enough to follow.

'It's not far, dear,' said Nettie. 'Nothing is, in a small town like this. But you take care now; no one's safe in Bradenford until the curse has run its course.'

'What if we don't believe in the curse?' I said.

Nettie gave me a pitying look. 'The curse doesn't care, dear. That's what's so terrible about it.'

Four
All Kinds of People Come to Church

There was no one out on the streets, apart from Penny and me. The narrow ways were completely deserted, and as we followed Nettie's directions to the church we didn't come into contact with another living soul. Penny kept turning her head restlessly, checking out every side street we passed, and glancing behind us as much as ahead. I kept my gaze fixed on what was in front of me. I knew we were alone; if there had been any other footsteps in the night I would have heard them. There was no traffic, nothing moving, and even our own footsteps sounded unnaturally loud on the quiet. As though the whole town was holding its breath, listening for something it was afraid of.

I wasn't scared. It's my job to make the monsters scared of me.

The street lights did their best to push back the darkness, but it still felt like we were walking through a ghost town. As though everyone else had run off and abandoned the streets to the night, for some very good reason. The only signs Bradenford was still inhabited lay in the lights that showed behind the drawn curtains of houses we passed. I felt like knocking on doors at random, and demanding to know what the hell was up with everyone. But I was pretty sure no one would answer. This was a town under siege; a town that believed in a curse. People so afraid for their lives that they stayed inside, behind locked doors, and hoped not to be noticed.

Curtains twitched now and again, from people curious to see who dared to walk their streets so openly at this time of the night. Penny waved cheerfully back whenever this happened, but there was never any response. So we just kept going, like children in a fairy-tale forest who really should have known better.

'Everyone seems to be taking this whole demonic threat thing extremely seriously,' said Penny, after a while.

'Maybe they know something we don't,' I said.

'Wouldn't be the first time,' said Penny. 'I'm starting to feel like I've got a target painted on my back.'

'You're safe,' I said. 'I'm here. And, there's no one else about.'

'That's what's worrying me,' said Penny. 'According to the story the demonic killer is invisible when it strikes.'

'I don't need to see it,' I said calmly. 'I'd still know it was there. I'd hear it coming, smell it on the air, feel its presence. That's what I do. And if it is stupid enough to come within arm's reach, I will stick my hand down its throat, grab hold of something solid and turn it inside out. And then stamp on it. No one gets to you while I'm around.'

'You say the sweetest things, darling,' said

Penny. She shot me a sideways look. 'You've been doing this weird and uncanny thing a lot longer than me. Are there really such things as demons?'

'OK . . .' I said. 'Demon is a word that covers a lot of unnatural territory. I've met a great many things that could pass for demons, but nothing I'd accept as something let loose from Hell. Whatever we come up against, remember the trick is to look it in the eye and not flinch.'

'You're really not reassuring me,' said Penny.

'If there actually is something to the Bergin family curse,' I said patiently, 'And I've yet to be convinced that there is . . . It's probably just some psychic residue left over from the original witch's death. A stone tape effect, perhaps; a stored memory being played back. Or possibly someone in the present being influenced by events in the past. All that really matters is that in order to have a physical effect, the attacker has to be physically present. And if anyone even looks at you funny I will punch them in the head so hard their brains will fly out of their ears.'

'Well,' said Penny. 'That's good to know.'

I looked at her. 'We've worked all kinds of cases together, and you've never been this jumpy before. What's wrong?'

'I don't know,' said Penny. 'It's this town. It feels like there's a shadow hanging over everything. Nothing I can point to, nothing I can give a name to . . . Just a feeling of something hiding, and waiting to jump out at us. Something that isn't right.'

'That's why we're here,' I said. 'To put things right.'

When we finally reached the church, it turned out to be the Norman building I'd spotted when we first drove through the town. A small sign on the rough stone wall said simply: *Trinity Church*.

'That's odd,' said Penny. 'Normally you'd expect to find a noticeboard giving details of the church's opening times, or at least a list of which services are available . . .'

'Maybe the church doesn't get used much,' I said.

'And maybe there's a good reason for that,' said Penny.

We stood back and looked the church over. It wasn't very big, with narrow, stained-glass windows and a bell tower topped with a spire complete with a brass weathercock, that was turning slowly back and forth as though trying to work out which way the wind was blowing. A slow chill went through me, as I realized there wasn't a breath of wind on the air. I pushed the thought aside. I couldn't let Penny's nerves get to me; I had a job to do. I made myself concentrate on the church.

'No lights on inside. Nothing to suggest anyone's at home.'

'The Reverend Allen was murdered here,' said Penny. 'That makes the church a crime scene.'

'Then why isn't it cordoned off?' I said. 'Why aren't there uniformed police standing around, to discourage people like us?'

'Maybe they're scared to be out at night, as well,' said Penny.

We went looking for the front door, and finally found it tucked away at the far end and round the corner. There was no one on guard, just a single length of yellow crime scene tape stretched across the door. I reached over the tape and tried the door. It was locked. At least someone had made an effort.

'It says on the tape: *Do Not Enter*,' Penny pointed out helpfully.

'I've always taken that as more of a suggestion,' I said.

I took a quick look around to make sure we weren't being observed, and then placed one hand on the door and broke the lock with one hard shove. The old wood splintered as the lock gave up the ghost and the door swung backwards, revealing nothing but a darkness that wasn't giving anything away.

'Show off,' said Penny.

We ducked under the police tape and slipped quietly into the church. I pushed the door shut behind us, but with the lock smashed it wouldn't stay closed. Penny and I stood still, staring into the gloom. I've always been able to see clearly in the dark, but I wanted to give Penny time for her eyes to adjust. It only took me a moment to establish we had the place to ourselves. I inhaled slowly, testing the scents on the still air. Polish and wax from the wooden pews, chemical cleaning agents from the floor, ghostly traces of long dead flowers, and a confused mess of human scents from recent visits. Along with a hell of a

79

lot of dust. I suppressed the urge to sneeze. I had a feeling the sound would carry.

'Can you smell blood?' Penny said quietly.

'No,' I said. 'But given that the vicar was found in the bell tower, I wouldn't expect to. How are your eyes doing?'

'Give me a minute,' she said. 'I'm only human.'

It wasn't that dark. Light from the street outside streamed in through the narrow, stained-glass windows, forming faded rainbows that cut though the dust-thick air to leave smeared colours on the stone floor. The shafts of light didn't spread, and the shadows all around were deep and dark, as though hiding ancient secrets. The hush that filled the church had an oppressive weight all of its own, as though it had been building for centuries. Prayer and song might dispel it for a while, but it would always return. Because it belonged here.

'I can see enough now,' said Penny. 'Though to be honest I have to say; for a church, it doesn't feel very welcoming.'

'You'd know better than me,' I said. 'As far as I'm concerned, a church is just one more place people go to do things I don't understand.'

'You're not religious?' said Penny. 'At all?'

I looked at her. 'You pick now to bring that up?'

'The subject never came up before. It's just that . . . with all the things we've encountered I always thought you must believe in something.'

'It's because I've seen so much, that I don't know what to believe,' I said. 'And besides, I never felt I'd belong in a place like this. Would the God of this church have room for something like me in its congregation?'

'I think so,' said Penny. 'I think that's the point.'

I didn't want to discuss it any further, so I set off down the aisle between the rows of wooden pews. Penny quickly caught up, and moved in close beside me.

'There are no cushions on the pews,' she said quietly. 'Even though that wood looks like it could prove really uncomfortable during a long service. And no pads to kneel on, despite the stone floor. Not even any prayer books set out . . . Apparently the Revered Allen provided a no-frills ministry.'

'Maybe he upset someone with that,' I said. 'There's nothing so divisive as a religious argument.'

We finally came to a halt before the simple altar. There was a huge cross on the wall above it, but no figure of Christ on the cross. Even I knew enough to find that unusual. Though given that this church dated back to Norman times, perhaps only the basics of the faith had survived.

'No flowers, no altar offerings,' said Penny. 'Not even any candles . . . It's all a bit bleak, isn't it? Especially considering there's going to be a wedding here tomorrow.'

'Most of what I know about church interiors comes from television,' I said. 'Since I don't do christenings, weddings or funerals. But even so, this doesn't feel right.'

'Maybe the police removed everything, as evidence,' said Penny.

I took another deep breath, and then looked sharply to my left. 'Someone died recently, not far from here.'

'Are you picking up blood now?' said Penny.

'And other bodily fluids,' I said. 'Death is always messy.'

'Oh ick.'

It didn't take us long to find the small side door that opened onto the bell tower; a simple stone chamber with no ceiling and a single hanging bell rope. I knelt down and studied the floor carefully. There were a few spots of blood, along with some other stains. Up close, I could even smell the chemical reagents the police scientists had used to confirm their identity.

'I can't see any stains,' said Penny. 'But then, in this gloom I can barely make out the floor.'

I gestured at the open door behind us. 'I think the Reverend Allen was killed somewhere in the church, and then dragged in here. There are definite scuff marks on the stone. And then the body was hauled over to the rope, and strung up.'

'To remind people of the hanged witch in the story.'

'Exactly.' I got to my feet and looked at the rope. 'It's always possible the killer meant to hang the vicar, but he struggled . . .'

'Either way, it doesn't sound very demonic, does it?' said Penny.

'No,' I said. 'The question is, what was the vicar hit with? A weapon, a trained hand, some convenient blunt instrument? And I suppose it's always possible one person struck down the vicar, and someone else put him on the rope to confuse the matter.'

'You think more than one person could be involved?'

'Possibly. And maybe for entirely separate reasons. But that's just a theory; there's no evidence to support it.'

'Lots of questions and no answers anywhere,' said Penny. 'A typical start to one of our cases.'

I took hold of the bell rope. Penny quickly put a hand on my arm.

'Really not a good idea,' she said. 'If this bell starts ringing again when no one's supposed to be in here, this town will lose its collective mind.'

I took my hand away. 'From the feel of it, the killer wouldn't have needed to pull the rope; just the vicar's weight would have been enough to get it started.' I stepped back, and took one last look around. 'No smell of brimstone, no scorch-marks from hellfire; so I think we can safely set aside demonic involvement.'

'I can never tell when you're joking,' said Penny. 'Let's get out of here. This place gives me the creeps.'

We went back into the main church. The quiet was so overwhelming I felt like stamping my feet down hard on the stone floor, just to prove I was there. Or even sing a few verses of 'The Good Ship Venus' as an act of defiance. I don't like being pressured; whether by people or an environment.

'So,' said Penny. 'What exactly have we

learned, from our completely unauthorized breaking and entering?'

'I don't buy the whole curse thing as a motive,' I said. 'I know the story says the demon will attack anyone who gets in its way, but this seems so . . . far removed.'

'Nettie said the curse didn't care,' said Penny. 'Maybe it just wants to scare people. And going by what's happening in the town, I'd have to say it's doing a good job. Even though we're a long way from the threatened slaughter on the wedding night.'

'Not going to happen,' I said firmly. 'I promised Robert.'

And then we both looked round. Someone was entering the church through the front door I hadn't been able to close.

'Someone's coming,' Penny said quietly.

'More than one,' I said. 'I'm picking up two distinct sets of footsteps.'

'OK,' said Penny. 'Definitely showing off now. What do we do?'

'Hang back and hide in the shadows, until we can tell who it is.'

Penny looked at me. 'You're not normally this cautious.'

'There's too much about this situation I don't understand. Do those footsteps sound demonic to you?'

'Oh shut up.'

We moved quietly into the deepest shadows we could find, beside the altar, and watched silently as a man and a woman made their way down the aisle between the pews. Passing in and out of the coloured shafts of light from the windows, and looking uncertainly about them. The young woman flashed her torch around every time she thought she heard something, which was pretty often, but the feeble beam didn't illuminate much. The young man sticking extremely close to her gave the strong impression of being not at all happy to be there. If he'd been any more tightly wound he wouldn't have been able to move. One loud sound and he'd probably jump right out of his skin. I was seriously tempted to shout '*Boo!*' just to see what would happen, but I didn't have a mop handy to clean up the mess afterwards.

Whoever these two people were, they weren't any kind of police. I waited till they stopped right in front of the altar, and then stepped smartly out of the shadows and into the light from the nearest window. The man let out a shrill shriek and dived behind his companion, who stood her ground and glowered at me challengingly.

'Who are you?' she said loudly. 'What are you doing here?'

'I could ask you the same question,' I said.

'I asked first! The public has a right to know . . .'

'Oh hell,' I said. 'You're the local reporter, aren't you?'

'Linda Meadows,' she said, just a bit defiantly. 'Investigative journalist for the *Bradenford Echo*. What gave me away?'

'Your attitude,' I said. 'Along with your being somewhere you know you're not supposed to be, and not giving a damn. And the fact that your companion is carrying a very professional-looking camera. Now turn your torch off before someone notices a light moving in here and reports it.'

Linda turned it off. Penny stepped forward into the light to stand beside me. The cameraman had just started emerging from behind Linda, but he immediately shrieked and ducked back again. Linda grabbed him by the ear and made him step out in the open. He jerked his head free, and sniffed sullenly.

'Don't like the dark,' he said loudly. 'Don't like deserted churches. Don't like murder scenes. Really don't like surprises.'

'You're in the wrong job then, aren't you?' Penny said kindly.

'This is my cameraman, Ian Adams,' said Linda. 'Don't mind him. I don't, except for when I'm forced to. Other women have cats or dogs; but he's good at his job so I'm stuck with him.'

'I stick with her because she's the only decent writer on the *Echo*,' said Ian. 'And because we've been friends ever since junior school. I worship the pointy shoes that walk all over me.'

'You stick with me because you know I'm going places,' said Linda. 'And I might just take you with me.'

'Isn't she wonderful?' said Ian.

I studied the two of them thoughtfully as they bickered. Linda was tall, blonde, and good-looking in a horsey sort of way. Mid-twenties, athletically slim, straight-backed and dressed to make a striking first impression. She had the air of someone ready to walk through walls to get where she was going. Ian was also in his mid-twenties, medium height, more than medium weight, and from the way he dressed clearly didn't give a damn about making any kind of impression. He had a round open face, curly red hair, and a sardonic grin that took the edge off his self-deprecating comments. He held his camera like a weapon, ready for use at any moment.

I introduced myself and Penny. Linda looked down her nose at us, to make it clear she'd never heard of us. There was enough nose involved to make that properly intimidating.

'What are you doing here?' she said.

'We're helping investigate the murder of the Reverend Allen,' I said. 'What are you doing, trespassing in a taped-off crime scene?'

Linda just shrugged, not in the least impressed by my assumed authority. 'Same as you, probably. Looking for answers. The police don't know a damned thing. Not that they had much of a chance to find out; they'd barely been here a few hours before they were all called away to deal with something more important. Inspector Godwin was the only one left behind.'

'Just one man, to cover a murder?' said Penny.

'I said that!' said Ian.

'Only after I said it first,' Linda said crushingly. 'It's obvious that something's going on.'

'You always say that,' said Ian.

'And I'm always right!' said Linda. 'Even if I can't always prove it. But I will get to the bottom of what's going on here; whatever it takes.'

'And she will,' Ian said proudly. 'Rely on it. No one can keep things from Linda. Mostly because everyone's too scared to lie to her.' He sniggered suddenly. 'That's how she got her job on the *Echo* in the first place; and why the editor doesn't dare fire her no matter who she upsets.'

'I am not scary!' Linda said loudly.

'I meant it in a nice way,' said Ian.

'Why is this story so important to you?' I said.

Linda didn't quite laugh in my face. 'Are you kidding me? A vicar hanged with his own bell rope, a family curse going back centuries, and a police investigation conspicuous by its absence? It's like being eaten alive by an Agatha Christie novel. If I play it right, this story will be my big break. My ticket out of here. I could ride this story all the way to a job on one of the nationals!' She stopped to glare at Ian. 'Don't screw this up, if you want to ride my coat-tails to the big time.'

'You provide the words, and I'll provide the things people really pay attention to,' Ian said happily.

'How can you write a story when there's hardly any facts?' said Penny.

'Easy,' said Linda. 'I'll just go gonzo on it, do the whole Hunter Thompson thing. Give our readers the full immersive experience, of how it feels to be a journalist fighting to get to the truth when the whole world is against you. This story isn't about facts anyway; it's about legends, and the people who believe in them. Which around here seems to be pretty much everyone. Did you see the streets out there? It's like the *Marie Celeste* on its lunch break. The whole town has lost its mind over the Bergin curse. I could fill pages, just describing how it feels to be in a deserted church at midnight (I know, dramatic license), and how people never came here while the vicar was alive, but since he was murdered you can't keep them out.'

'That's sad,' said Ian.

'That's news,' said Linda. 'If this murder scene was any more popular, someone would be selling tickets.'

'It's not like there's anything here to see,' said Ian. 'I mean; if they'd left the vicar on the rope I could have got a dynamite photo . . .' He broke off as we all looked at him. 'Except, of course, that would be wrong. And insensitive. I never thought that even for a moment.'

Linda shrugged. 'Give the public what it wants and they'll line up just to get a glimpse of it. As long as it's daylight. The moment it started getting dark they were fighting each other to get out of here and run off home.'

'You know this town,' I said. 'Were there any scandals, or rumours, attached to the Reverend Allen?'

'Nothing you could point an investigative stick at,' said Linda. 'Everyone I spoke to said pretty much the same thing; well-meaning, but dull. Getting murdered was the most exciting thing he ever did.'

'Do you believe in the Bergin family curse?' said Penny.

'I'm ready to believe in anything that will sell papers,' said Linda. 'If the curse is what people want to read about, then that's what I'll write.'

'Why are you working for a newspaper?' I said. 'I thought it was all blogs these days?'

Linda shook her head firmly. 'Everyone and their pet dog is writing a blog, so if you want to stand out, if you want people to pay attention, you need a platform. And newspapers are still the best way to back up your stories with the appearance of authority. Print has impact, and permanence if you get it right. Blogs are amateur night; and I've never been one to settle for second best.'

'But do you believe in the curse?' I said. 'Do you think that's what's happening here?'

'Well . . .' said Linda.

'The original murders were real enough,' said Ian. 'You can read all about them in the *Echo*'s archives. Two dead at wedding, and summary justice straight afterwards. Everyone who grows up here gets force-fed the story with their mother's milk. So it's hardly surprising that . . .'

He broke off as he realized Linda was glaring at him.

'Aren't we the Chatty Cathy all of a sudden?' she said loudly. 'I do the words, Danny; you stand back and point your camera.' She turned her glare on me. 'What about you? Do you believe some ancient demon hung the vicar with his own bell rope, just to send a message?'

'I don't see any evidence of a demonic presence,' I said carefully. 'What evidence there is points to a human killer.'

'Finally!' said Linda. 'Another sane person!' She looked at Ian. 'And no, you don't count because you still read your horoscope in the

Echo; even after I told you I write them, and it all depends on what mood I'm in.'

'Typical Sagittarius,' said Ian.

'I will slap you and it will hurt,' said Linda.

'Try not to leave a visible bruise this time,' said Ian.

Linda dismissed him with a loud sniff, and turned her full attention on me. 'Who exactly are you working for?'

'Even if I told you, you wouldn't be allowed to publish it,' I said. 'And no you can't quote me on that, or anything else. Because officially, I'm not here.'

'Oh . . .' said Linda. 'One of those.'

'What?' said Ian.

'He's hinting, with all the subtlety of a flying half brick, that he's something to do with security,' said Linda. 'See if you can get a photo of him, before he disappears back into the shadows.'

Ian started to raise his camera, and then stopped as he took in the look on my face. He lowered the camera and shrugged apologetically at Linda.

'I don't think he wants his photo taken.'

'Who's in charge here?' said Linda.

'As long as he's looking at me like that, he is,' said Ian.

Linda decided it was time to change tactics, and gave me what she probably thought was her best beguiling look. 'Come on. Mister Jones; I won't name you, or say what you're doing here. You can be just . . . an interested observer. Most people love to have their photo in the paper.'

'I'm not most people,' I said.

'That's true,' Penny said smoothly. 'He really

91

isn't. You can take a photo of me if you want. I'm not anyone important.'

Linda looked at her. 'Yes . . . You're young and pretty. Mystery woman investigates family curse. That's a good headline; for an inside page. Do it, Ian.'

Ian looked at me, to make sure I was OK with that, and once I'd moved carefully out of range he took several quick photos of Penny as she smiled and posed obligingly. The flashes from Ian's camera lit the church bright as day, and for a moment it seemed like just another building. I had to wait till everyone else had stopped blinking, before I could ask more questions.

'Do you know where the vicar's body was taken?' I said.

'The ambulance men said they'd been told to take him to the mortuary at Upper Torley,' said Ian. 'That's the neighbouring town. They're big enough to have a proper hospital.'

'Why are you interested in the body?' said Linda. 'Do you want to check it for demonic traces? Perform an exorcism?'

'I'm more interested in exactly how the vicar's neck was broken, before he was strung up,' I said. 'You did know about that?'

'I did,' said Linda. 'I didn't know you did.'

'Ambulance men love to talk,' said Ian.

'Some person killed the Reverend Allen,' I said. 'Not vengeance from beyond the grave. You know of any strangers in town?'

'Like you?' said Linda.

I smiled. 'Stranger than me.'

Linda shrugged. 'There's a few staying at The

Swan, here for the wedding. I've spoken to them. Apparently the rest of the guests aren't expected until tomorrow. But that's about it, for new faces.'

'Did you know the wedding is still going ahead tomorrow?' said Penny. 'Right here, despite everything?'

'That's what they told me!' said Linda. 'I couldn't believe it. Actually the bride to be told me, and the groom just nodded. Easy to see who wears the trousers in that relationship.' She looked at Ian. 'Did you say something?'

'Who, me?' Ian said innocently. 'I wouldn't dare.'

'Getting married here, after everything that's happened, struck me as more than a bit creepy,' said Linda. 'I mean, taking your vows just yards from where the man who was to marry you went to meet his maker way ahead of schedule?'

'Love is blind,' said Ian. 'Or in this case, perhaps a little short-sighted.'

'Will you be covering the wedding?' said Penny.

'Oh yes,' Linda said airily. 'Tom Stone may not be a star, or even a celebrity as such, but he's appeared on television; and that's enough to put him on the front page of the *Echo*. Under the fold, of course; the murder still takes precedence.' She turned to Ian, 'The editor will probably want a full centre spread as well, so be sure to get plenty of photos. And if the bride gives you a hard time, feel free to shoot her from the most unflattering angles you can find.'

'I can do that,' said Ian.

'Normally the *Echo* is just a weekly,' Linda

93

said to me and Penny. 'But we're putting out daily editions for as long as the excitement lasts. Small town papers live for moments like this. People will lose interest in the curse once the wedding is over and no one else has died; but until then we make money while the sun shines.'

'Unless there are more deaths,' I said.

'Oh, that would be amazing!' said Linda. 'If this should turn out to be a serial killer, this story would run and run! We're talking book contracts, movie deals . . .'

'She's not actually heartless,' said Ian. 'Just very focused on her job.'

And then we all looked round sharply, as someone else entered the church through the front door. Not even trying to make a secret of it. We all drew together instinctively, at the prospect of a common enemy.

'For a deserted church, this place is getting a lot of traffic tonight,' I said.

'Stay where you are!' said a loud voice from the other end of the church. 'This is Detective Inspector Godwin! I know you're here, I saw your lights. This is a restricted area; show yourselves.'

Penny looked at me. 'What do you want to do?'

'Talk to the man,' I said. 'See what he knows that we don't.'

'We're not official,' said Penny.

'He doesn't know that.'

'You're not official?' said Linda.

'There's official, and then there's official,' I said.

'Is there a back door to this place?' said Ian. 'I think I hear my mother calling me.'

'Stop panicking!' said Linda. 'We have every right to be here.'

'No, we don't!' said Ian. 'He told us specifically not to come back, after he caught us sneaking in with the last bunch of murder groupies.'

'The public has a right to know!'

'He didn't seem to believe that.'

'Are you more afraid of him, or me?' said Linda.

Ian looked at the dark figure striding down the aisle toward us, flashing a torch ahead of him.

'Well?' said Linda.

'Don't rush me,' said Ian. 'I'm thinking.'

'I can hear you talking!' said Inspector Godwin. 'Stay right where you are!'

'He sounds just a bit angry,' said Penny.

'He always does,' said Ian. 'Probably came out of the womb accusing the midwife of wasting police time.'

'You can always hide behind me,' said Linda. 'Peter knows better than to pull that crap with me.'

Godwin finally slammed to a halt before us, shining his torch right into our faces. I didn't flinch at the bright light, but the others had to turn their faces away. Godwin was just a dark figure behind the light, an imposing and authoritative presence; which was almost certainly the point. I raised my voice before he could raise his.

'Get that light out of my face.'

'I'm in charge here,' said Godwin.

'I wouldn't put money on it,' I said. 'It's up

95

to you; lose the torch or wave goodbye to your career prospects.'

Godwin reacted instinctively to the casual authority in my voice, and turned off his torch. I was finally able to get a good look at him. Detective Inspector Godwin was a lot younger than he sounded; only in his mid-twenties. Medium height, in good shape, and good-looking in a rough and ready kind of way. His plain clothes looked like he'd slept in them, and had a really restless night. He scowled at me.

'Who are you? Identify yourself!'

'I am Ishmael Jones, and this is Penny Belcourt. Here for the wedding of Robert Bergin's daughter. He and I used to work for the same people. I'm told you're the only police presence in this town. Where is everyone?'

'There's been a major industrial accident, two towns over,' said Godwin. 'All the fire, police and ambulance services from across the county have been called to attend. Until that's dealt with everything else takes a back seat. I'm all they could spare to keep an eye on things here.'

'Why you?' said Penny.

'Because I grew up in the town,' said Godwin. 'I'm supposed to have local insight into the community.'

'You know about the Bergin curse?' I said.

He shrugged uncomfortably. 'It's just a story, something the town can use to sell tatt to tourists.' He broke off, to glare at Linda and Ian. 'I told you to stay out of here! This is a crime scene!'

'Technically, the bell tower is the crime scene,' I said.

'I don't take kindly to being corrected,' said Godwin.

'Then your life must be full of disappointments,' I said.

He didn't quite know how to take that. 'What authority do you have to be here? Who are you working for, exactly? I think it's time I saw some ID.'

'Not going to happen,' I said easily. 'People like us don't carry ID.'

'I knew it,' Godwin said bitterly. 'You're one of Bergin's mob. Licensed to get in everyone's way.'

'You know who Robert worked for?' I said, not quite raising an eyebrow.

'I made some enquiries,' said Godwin. 'And given from how far up the order came to stop doing that, I drew my own conclusions.'

Linda was fascinated by all of this, looking from Godwin to me and back again. Though she had enough sense not to interrupt and draw attention to herself.

'What's your interest in this case?' said Godwin.

'We're just here for the wedding,' I said. 'And to help out an old friend.'

'That old man has serious connections,' said Godwin. 'I wasn't even allowed to talk to him. But remember; this is still a police operation! We don't need or want any help from outsiders.'

'Perish the thought,' I said.

I nodded to Penny, and we strode past Godwin without even looking at him. Linda and Ian hurried after us, giving Godwin plenty of room.

97

We'd almost made it to the front door when Godwin suddenly yelled after us.

'How did you get in here? That door was locked!'

'It isn't now,' I said, not looking back.

Once we were all out in the street, Linda and Ian exchanged relieved glances and took a moment to get their breath back.

'We were really lucky to get away with that,' said Linda. 'Peter takes his job very seriously.'

'You mean he likes to throw his authority around,' said Ian.

'You know him?' said Penny.

'Oh sure,' said Ian. 'We went to school together.'

'Peter always wanted to be a cop,' said Linda. 'Though I think he's finding the reality a bit different from what he expected.'

'He was a bully at school too,' said Ian.

'You have to remember what his father was like,' said Linda.

Ian nodded, reluctantly. 'Hardly a day when Peter didn't turn up at school without a fresh set of cuts and bruises. They had to take him to the hospital twice.'

'I think that's why he worked so hard to become a policeman,' said Linda. 'So he could stop people like his father from doing the kind of things his father did.'

'And then the old bastard died of a heart attack, before Peter could put him away,' said Ian. 'Life isn't fair.'

'No, it isn't,' said Linda. 'That's why we need

police. And good investigative reporters. You have to make allowances for Peter.'

'No I bloody don't,' said Ian. 'I had bruises of my own, because of him.'

Linda looked at me thoughtfully. 'What was Peter talking about, when he said Mr Bergin had connections?'

'Best not to ask,' I said briskly.

'Are we talking real Security here?' said Linda.

'You might be,' I said. 'I'm not.'

'You're some kind of spy?' said Ian, finally catching up with the rest of us.

'Certainly not,' I said. 'And don't believe anyone who tells you otherwise. They're only guessing.'

'I will find out,' said Linda. 'That's what I do.'

'We're just here for the wedding,' Penny said sweetly. 'Nice to meet you both. Come along, Ishmael.'

We walked away. Behind us, I could hear Linda and Ian arguing quietly. She was trying to get him to sneak a photo of me, and he was having none of it. She might wear the trousers but he had more survival instincts.

'Well,' said Penny, linking her arm through mine as we strolled along. 'I think we muddied the waters there nicely, but I don't know how much more bluffing we can get away with.'

'Enough to keep them running around in circles, while we get on with the investigation,' I said.

'You don't think Godwin will go and bother Robert now his superiors aren't here to stop him, do you?' said Penny. 'He seemed very determined.'

'He'll get short shrift from Robert if he does,' I said. 'Robert really does have connections. More than enough to put a muzzle on Godwin.'

'I liked the way you implied you were here representing Black Heir, without actually confirming it,' said Penny.

'If Godwin tries to follow up on that, he'll end up even more confused,' I said.

'But I'm not sure we learned anything useful,' said Penny.

'We now know why the streets are so deserted,' I said. 'And why there isn't a proper police presence.'

'But we're no nearer working out who killed the Reverend Allen, or whether Gillian and Tom are in any real danger.'

'No,' I said. 'We're not. I think we need to talk to Gillian and Tom again. When you want to catch a predator, bait a trap and watch the bait.'

'You mean you want to use Gillian and Tom? That's a bit cold-blooded, isn't it?' said Penny.

'Not if I'm really angry with the predator when it turns up,' I said.

Penny stirred uncomfortably. 'We need to be a bit careful here, Ishmael. We don't have the Organization's backing on this case.'

'You never cared about that before.'

'This feels different.'

I didn't have anything to say to that. Because she was right; it did.

Five
Nothing Stays Secret Forever

'So,' said Penny, as we made our way down the deserted street. 'Where are we going now?'

'Back to The Swan,' I said. 'First, because I think we need to sit down somewhere quiet and read the books Robert gave us, on the Bergin curse. We don't know nearly enough about the details, and the background. If we take a book each and skip the boring bits, we should get through them fast enough. And second; we need to talk to Gillian and Tom again. I want to know why it's so important that they get married tomorrow. Why can't they wait?'

'Marriages take a lot of planning,' said Penny. 'And involve a lot of people. It could be very expensive, as well as inconvenient, to call it all off at such short notice. But even so . . . to insist on getting married in a church where someone just got killed? That is seriously creepy.'

'Gillian and Tom are keeping things from us,' I said. 'And I need to know what they are.'

'Might not be anything to do with the murder, or the curse,' said Penny.

'It's to do with something,' I said.

The evening was almost painfully quiet, like the whole town was waiting for the other shoe to drop. There was still no traffic on the road, not even a passing bus or taxi. The street was completely deserted, with not a sign of life anywhere, and there was a distinct chill on the air, as though autumn had come early while we weren't watching. I stopped suddenly, and looked sharply around me. Penny stopped too, and peered quickly up and down the street. It was all very still, nothing moving anywhere.

'All right,' Penny said quietly. 'What am I missing? I don't see anything.'

'Neither do I,' I said. 'I'm not hearing anything, either. But I can't shake the feeling that we're not alone. That we're being watched, by unfriendly eyes.'

Penny moved in close beside me. Not because she was worried, but so we could stand together if we needed to defend ourselves. Her eyes were flashing angrily, and her hands had closed into fists. I had to smile. I've always been able to depend on Penny to back me up.

'Could it be the invisible demon?' she said. 'I really don't like the idea of something I can't see sneaking up on me. You said you'd know if it was around. Do you think it's here with us, now?'

'I don't know,' I said. 'It just feels like something's here. Something so close it's breathing down my neck.'

'Something bad?' said Penny.

'I don't know! But . . . it's like I'm afraid to take a step in any direction in case that's the wrong thing to do.'

I was so tense my back muscles were aching.

102

My heart pumped painfully hard in my chest, and I had trouble getting my breath. I glared up and down the empty street, again and again, looking for something, anything, out of place. But there was nothing, nothing at all. Penny stirred restlessly.

'Look, whatever it is, we can't just stand around here. Let's get moving. The hotel is just down the end of the street and round the corner. Come on, Ishmael; we can be there in a few minutes.'

She put an arm through mine and urged me forward. The first step was hard, but once we were moving it got easier. We walked quickly down the street, striding it out. I thought our sudden movement might flush whatever was hiding into revealing itself, but the street remained empty. And slowly, I began to understand what had just happened. That feeling of some inhuman enemy watching wasn't something on the street; it was something inside me. My old self, rising to the surface once again. Whatever chains had held it down for so long were finally weakening. It had manifested just long enough to look out at the world through my eyes; and then it sank back down again. But not because of anything I'd done.

I didn't tell Penny. I didn't want her to be scared of me. Of what I used to be. Of the monster that had been hiding behind my face, all these years. It had always been my greatest fear, that Penny would be hurt because of me.

We burst into the hotel lobby like travellers in

peril, grateful to find themselves in a safe haven at last. We stumbled to a halt, and then leaned heavily on each other as we got our breath back. Nettie was still on duty at the reception desk. She sat up straight as we entered, one hand rising automatically to pat at her wig and make sure it was properly in place. She gave us a moment to recover our composure, and then hit Penny and me with her best professional smile.

'Back so soon, dears?'

I gave her my best *everything's fine nothing to worry about here* smile. 'We'd like to use the bar, if that's all right.'

'Of course; you go right ahead, dears,' said Nettie. 'You might as well make use of it; no one else is. But I'm afraid Albert won't be there to serve you. He had one of his heads, so I said he could take a break until he felt better. And I can't leave the desk . . .'

'We just want to do some quiet reading,' said Penny.

'Oh, that's nice, dear. Help yourself to a drink if you want; just leave the money on the bar top. I wouldn't bother the till; it doesn't like strangers. It isn't that fond of people it knows . . .'

We left her still chattering and went into the bar. It was completely empty. No Albert, no customers, nothing.

'There's something sad about a bar with no one in it,' I said. 'Not unlike a church no one can be bothered to attend.'

Penny looked at me. 'Why would that upset you? You're not religious.'

'I'm not,' I said. 'But I like to think other people are. And bars should definitely have people in them. That's what bars are for.'

'Do you want a drink?' said Penny.

'Not just now.'

'Then I won't either.'

We sat down at the first table we came to, and I fished the two paperback books out of my jacket pockets.

'Which do you want?' I said.

Penny immediately made a grab for the one with the Gothic romance artwork. *The Bergin Curse*, by Jason Grant. I took the other; *A Bloodline Of Murder*, by Paul Hoch. Both books looked very well read, as though Robert had been through them from end to end more than once. Looking for clues, or loopholes. Penny and I settled ourselves comfortably, and started reading.

My book was more interested in journalism than sensationalism, concentrating on what facts there were, and keeping the jumping to conclusions to a minimum. It started by covering the original murders very thoroughly. On the 15th of July, 1783, on a pleasant day of more than usually calm weather, most of the better-off in the county gathered to witness the marriage of Elizabeth Bergin to Joseph Heartley. Two very well known and very well thought of young people. It was a delightful day and a lovely ceremony; until the spurned Susan Glenn burst into the church and attacked the happy couple, hacking them to death with a butcher's knife. Half the congregation surged forward to drag her away from her victims, but they were too late. Covered in blood and laughing hysterically, Susan Glenn spat in the faces of those who held her, defying any of them to put right the awful thing she'd done.

She was hanged on the orders of the bride's father, Nathanial Bergin; though it wasn't recorded that anyone objected.

In the seventy years that followed, the grooms of four more Bergin brides died suddenly on their wedding nights. Details on these deaths were somewhat scarcer. After that, the Bergin line produced only sons, bringing the unexplained murders to an end. The legend of the Bergin curse grew down the years, mostly thanks to local people who saw it as a way to bring in the tourists. But interestingly, the Bergin curse wasn't the only supernatural event attached to the town of Bradenford. The book spent some time detailing a series of bloody deaths that occurred in and around the town, at roughly the same time as the first Bergin murders. Several men and women were torn to pieces, their deaths attributed at first to a wild animal, and then . . . to a werewolf. No one was ever caught, or even accused, and in time the murders just stopped. Lacking the romantic underpinnings of the Bergin curse, the werewolf story was soon forgotten outside the local area.

The book's author didn't try to link the two stories together; he just seemed to be commenting on the fact that people in Bradenford had a taste for supernatural stories.

I put the book down, and thought about it. Could

the invisible demonic killer have its basis in a werewolf; never caught in the act because it was able to disappear back into its unsuspected human host? But then, why would a werewolf target just the husbands of Bergin brides? None of the other werewolf killings seemed in any way connected to the family. And after all, a bride and groom wouldn't have been likely to invite anyone into their home on their wedding night. Unless it was family . . . I shook my head. Accepting the werewolf story just complicated the situation. I looked across at Penny.

'How are you doing?'

She tossed her book onto the table. 'It's a bit hard going. Reads more like a novel than a history. One of those cheap Gothic melodramas, dripping with mood but lacking in plot, featuring a heroine with absolutely no common sense. The author all but accuses Elizabeth Bergin of bringing it on herself, for accepting a proposal from a man who'd already dumped one woman. He also hints very strongly that Joseph Heartley only married Elizabeth Bergin for her money.' Penny frowned. 'There's no evidence in the book to suggest that Susan Glenn really was a witch. Just a lot of contemporary gossip, and after the fact myth-making. But of course back then any woman on her own was fair game, and could be accused of witchcraft for all kinds of reasons.'

'Is there anything in your book about werewolves?' I said.

Penny looked at me. 'If there is, I haven't got to it yet. Werewolves? Really? Aren't things complicated enough as it is?'

'I thought that. And anyway, a werewolf would have torn the Reverend Allen to pieces, not killed him in such a cold and calculated fashion. I still can't see why the vicar was targeted in the first place.'

'Maybe the point of it was to intimidate Gillian and Tom into calling off their wedding,' said Penny. 'But . . . why would anyone go to such lengths to do that?'

'We need to talk to the happy couple again,' I said, getting to my feet. 'You wait here a moment.'

'Is it OK if I skip to the end of this thing?' said Penny.

'It's your book,' I said.

I went back into the lobby, and Nettie perked up immediately. Apparently I was the only interesting thing happening that evening.

'Anything I can do to help, dear?'

'Could you phone Gillian and Tom in their room, and ask them to come down and join us in the bar?' I said. 'It's rather urgent.'

'Of course, dear. Not a problem.' She reached for the phone, and then stopped. 'Or is it a problem? Is this anything I should be concerned about?'

'It's just some last-minute wedding details that need sorting out,' I said. 'There's always something . . .'

'Of course, dear,' said Nettie. 'The whole town's looking forward to the wedding tomorrow. One of our own, marrying a television star! And I'm looking forward to hosting the wedding reception, at the church hall afterwards. It's a pity the guests won't be staying in the hotel overnight, but . . . We'll put on a nice buffet for them; locally-sourced produce, all of it; even if it is just stand up and fingers.'

I looked meaningfully at the telephone, and she stopped talking and picked it up. I went back into the bar and sat down opposite Penny.

'Gillian and Tom will be here soon.'

'Why do you always put her name first?' said Penny.

I raised an eyebrow. 'Have you met them?'

Penny nodded. 'How much do you think we should tell them, about what we know that they don't?'

'Like what?' I said.

'Well, the demon and the werewolf, for starters. Robert's back history with Black Heir, and the Hazard Asylum,' said Penny. 'Any of which could be connected to the Reverend Allen's murder.'

'I think the key words there are "could be",' I said. 'There's no point in worrying them unnecessarily. I'm more interested in what they know that we don't.'

'But . . .'

'We have no evidence that anything unnatural is going on here,' I said.

'But don't they have a right to know all the possibilities, if their lives are in danger?' said Penny.

'The only real possibility of an outside threat comes from Robert's past,' I said. 'And when it comes to talking about Black Heir, that has to be his decision. There must be a reason why he

109

never mentioned any of that to his daughter.'

We both looked round quickly as Gillian and Tom entered the bar, along with Robert. Penny and I rose to our feet, and there was a brief flurry of smiles and handshakes.

'I couldn't just sit around on my own, doing nothing,' Robert said gruffly. 'I've been trying to talk these young idiots into postponing the wedding. Everyone would understand. But, they're having none of it.' He looked at the paperbacks on the table, and nodded slowly. 'I've been talking to them about that, as well. There is a sort of epilogue to the legend, though you may not have got to it yet. If the bride and groom can survive long enough to get married, and make it through the wedding night unharmed, then the Bergin curse will be broken forever. Though that's never happened, so far.'

'You didn't bring the best man and bridesmaid with you,' Penny said to Gillian and Tom. 'I was looking forward to meeting them.'

'The message only said you wanted to speak to us,' said Gillian. 'So we didn't disturb them. You'll see them tomorrow, at the wedding.'

'If we get through tonight,' said Tom. 'My nerves are so on edge . . .'

Gillian smiled at him. 'When we get back to our room, I'll do that thing you like.'

Tom brightened up. 'The thing I really like?'

'Well, I like it too,' said Gillian.

'That should help pass the time,' said Tom.

Robert cleared his throat loudly, to remind them he was still there. I invited everyone to sit down, and we all drew up chairs around the

110

table. I put the two books back in my pockets, for later. Everyone was looking at me expectantly so I dived right in.

'Do either of you have any enemies?' I said bluntly to Gillian and Tom. 'Anyone who might not want your wedding to take place?'

'No,' Gillian said immediately.

Tom nodded quickly. 'That was the first thing Robert suggested, but before this I would have said we didn't have an enemy in the world.'

I glanced at Robert, but he didn't say anything.

'Why is it so important that the wedding has to go ahead tomorrow?' said Penny. 'Why not just live together, until you can make new arrangements?'

'I said that!' said Tom. And then he looked quickly at Gillian. 'I know you have your heart set on this . . .'

'No,' said Gillian. 'It's a fair question. Do I have the right to put you in danger, just to fulfil a fantasy I had as a teenager?'

'If this is what you want . . .' said Tom.

'I'm not so sure I do, now,' said Gillian. 'The dream's been spoiled. We could forget the whole idea of getting married . . .'

'Absolutely not,' Tom said firmly. 'We are getting married tomorrow, as planned. The more everything conspires to stop us, the more determined I am not to be stopped. I know how much this means to you, it's all you've talked about for months; and I won't have you cheated out of it. You are going to have your dream wedding and I won't let anyone or anything spoil it for you.'

Gillian beamed at him. 'Isn't he wonderful?'

They clasped hands across the tabletop. And while they were lost in each other, Robert caught my eye.

'If I could just have a quick word in private, Ishmael?'

'Of course,' I said.

We got to our feet. Gillian and Tom looked at us sharply.

'What's this?' said Gillian. 'Secrets?'

'Just something we need to get sorted out between us,' said Robert. 'Won't be a minute.'

'Why can't we hear what it is?' said Tom.

'Because it's private,' said Robert.

He led the way to a table on the far side of the bar. As far away from the others as we could get without actually leaving the room. He sat down with his back to Gillian and Tom, who were still staring after us curiously. I sat down facing Robert.

'All right,' I said quietly. 'What is it you want to talk about that can't be said in front of your daughter, or the man she's going to marry?'

Robert looked searchingly at my face, studying it carefully, as though hoping to find some sign of age or change that had escaped him before. And when he couldn't, he just sighed briefly and sat back in his chair.

'You look exactly the way I remember you. As though not a day has passed. Whatever you've got, I want some.'

'No,' I said. 'You don't.'

He wasn't convinced. 'I got old, and you didn't.'

'You have a family, and I don't,' I said.

'Family . . .' said Robert. 'It's always about family. I thought I'd left all the weird stuff behind me when I retired from Black Heir. I never told Gillian anything about the life I used to lead, and I'd be obliged if you wouldn't mention it either. Helen and I decided a long time ago that we didn't want Gillian to know anything about that side of the world. So she'd never have to worry about it.'

'We might have to tell her, at some point,' I said.

'If we do, I'll decide when and how much,' said Robert.

'As you wish,' I said.

'I haven't told the police anything about what I used to do,' said Robert. 'Because I don't trust them to keep it to themselves. They know I've got connections, and that's all they need to know. But . . . I can't ask Black Heir for help. They've always made a point of never operating in the public eye. You're my last hope, Ishmael.' He looked down at his old hands, clasped together on the tabletop. 'Helen and I broke off all contact with Black Heir, once we retired. To make sure Gillian would never know about the kind of nightmares we used to deal with. We wanted her to have a normal life. So we didn't keep in touch with any of our old friends, not even people we'd been close to for decades. And we made it very clear we weren't interested in hearing from anyone, under any circumstances. A bit cold, perhaps, but family has to come first. Did you keep in touch with anyone, after you left?'

'No,' I said. 'I had even more reasons than you to cut all ties.'

Robert smiled briefly. 'I won't ask.'

'Best not to,' I said.

'Did you ever bump into anyone, afterwards?'

I looked at him for a moment, wondering where this was going. 'Just the once. I met Alexander Khan, a few years back. You remember him.'

'Oh aye,' said Robert. 'Left Black Heir to go into business, didn't he? Something to do with communications . . . Whatever happened to him?'

'He died,' I said.

Robert looked at me sharply. 'You didn't . . .'

'No,' I said. 'I found out who killed him, and put an end to them.'

'Of course you did,' said Robert. 'I'm sorry, Ishmael, it's just . . . It's been so long since I last spoke to you. People change. Well, I did . . .' And then he stopped, and looked at me seriously.

And I thought: *This is it. Here it comes.*

'I need to talk to you,' Robert said steadily. 'About Hazard Asylum.'

'Good,' I said. 'I've been wondering about that. Is it possible that this could be your past catching up with you? Could someone have escaped from the Asylum, and tracked you here?'

'No,' said Robert. 'That's not possible.'

'How can you be so sure?'

'That's what I need to tell you,' he said. 'I never wanted you to know this, Ishmael; but I can't afford for you to be distracted, chasing a false trail.' He stopped for a moment, as though

114

bracing himself. 'Hazard Asylum isn't what you think it is. You don't have to worry about some inmate getting out; because no one has ever been held at the Asylum.'

'What are you talking about?' I said. 'You escorted dozens of people there. I saw the paperwork.'

'It was decided long ago, at the highest levels of Black Heir, that there was no point in locking up people who'd been damaged by alien contact,' Robert said heavily. 'There was nothing we could do to cure them, or even ease their pain; and there was always the chance they might escape and hurt someone else. So we killed them. We killed all of them.'

He nodded slowly, unflinchingly, as he took in the look on my face.

'That look, right there, is why I never told you. Why I took pains to make sure you were never involved with that side of things. I knew you wouldn't approve. That you couldn't cope, with what had to be done. You have to understand, Ishmael; it was the only way to put an end to their suffering.'

'How many of these people did you kill?' I said.

'Oh, that wasn't me,' said Robert. 'I just took them to the Asylum, like a good little Judas goat at a slaughterhouse. Told them everything would be fine, and then handed them over to people who killed them quickly and humanely. And destroyed the bodies afterwards, so there'd be nothing left of them.'

He stopped again, to see how I was taking it.

And I thought, but didn't say: *No wonder you didn't want Gillian to know . . .*

I wasn't sure how I felt. I could see the implacable logic behind the decision, I'd seen how badly damaged some of those people had been; but still the sheer cold-bloodedness of it appalled me. I wondered if I'd ever suspected the truth, on some level. If I'd heard things, put two and two together without realizing it, and that was why I'd had nightmares about being taken to Hazard Asylum. Had I not allowed myself to know? No. I'd never even suspected; because if I had I'd have done . . . something.

'I never knew anything about this,' I said.

'Not many did,' said Robert. 'It was our burden to carry. We saw no reason to impose it on others. I'm not asking for your forgiveness, Ishmael, or even your understanding. I came to terms with what I did long ago. I just need you to understand that there is no possibility of the murderer being connected to the Asylum.'

'How could you do it?' I said. 'How could you escort so many people to their deaths?'

'It was necessary,' he said. 'If you could have seen the condition of some of them, it would have broken your heart. Dying by inches, driven out of their minds . . . But that was the main reason why I stopped doing fieldwork. Something like that . . . it wears on the soul. I wanted you to know this, because Gillian must never know. She must never find out the kind of man her father used to be.'

'I don't see any reason to tell her,' I said. 'But that could change. You haven't thought this

116

through, Robert. What if one of these damaged people had a relative, or a loved one, who discovered the truth? What if someone decided you needed to pay, by losing someone you love?'

'No one ever knew!' said Robert. 'That was the point!'

'Nothing stays secret forever,' I said.

Six
Losing Control

The bar felt suddenly overcrowded as Detective Inspector Godwin strode in. Gillian, Tom and Penny rose immediately to their feet to face him, as though just his presence made them feel like they were being accused of something. Robert and I took our time getting to our feet, and then moved over to join the others. Just in case it became necessary to present a unified front in the face of a common enemy. Godwin stood his ground and looked at all of us unflinchingly, as though he was used to that kind of reaction. In fact, he seemed almost pleased, taking it as a compliment and an acknowledgment of his authority. At least he had the good sense not to smile.

'I'm here to talk to the happy couple again,' he said. 'Though of course I'm happy to see you, Mr Bergin.' He turned to look at me and Penny. 'What are you doing in The Swan?'

'Standing here, talking to you,' I said. 'Are you following us around, Inspector? If I'd known you were that interested I'd have done something entertaining.'

'Should I be following you?' said Godwin.

'Of course not,' Penny said quickly. 'We're no one special. Just guests, here for the wedding.'

She gave me a hard look. I know I shouldn't

tease Godwin, but there was just something about the man that got on my nerves. Charging around interrogating everyone, refusing to take no for an answer; who did he think he was? Me?

'What are you doing here, Peter?' said Robert.

'Inspector Godwin, please, Mr Bergin, when I'm on duty. I'm here because I still have a few questions that need answering. Perhaps you would prefer your guests to leave, before I begin.'

'How do you know Ishmael and Penny?' said Robert.

'I caught them sneaking around the church, without permission,' said Godwin.

'Is it really sneaking, if we're the ones who caught you off guard?' I said.

'Don't get smart with me,' said Godwin.

'OK, now you're just taunting me with feed lines,' I said.

Penny put a warning hand on my arm, and squeezed hard. 'Play nicely, darling. The inspector is only doing his job.'

She was reminding me that we had no official standing, and no backup from the Organization.

Gillian looked at me curiously. 'What were you doing in the church?'

'Making sure it was safe for you, for tomorrow,' said Penny. She moved quickly to change the subject. 'We met someone else there who said they knew you: Linda and Ian?'

'Oh, them,' said Gillian.

'Who?' said Tom.

'Local reporter and her pet cameraman,' said Robert. 'They mean well. I suppose.'

'Oh God,' said Tom. 'They're going to want

119

an interview, aren't they? I'd better come with a few anecdotes about people they've heard of, if we want to see some decent wedding photos in the local paper.'

'I don't think that'll be a problem,' I said. 'Small-town papers love a celebrity with a local connection.'

'You two should leave,' said Godwin, sensing the conversation was moving away from him. 'I have questions to ask the family that are none of your business.'

'I'd rather they stayed,' Robert said immediately. 'They're close friends.'

'I thought we'd already answered all your questions,' said Tom. 'What more do you need to know?'

'Just a few facts I need to get straight,' said Godwin.

Gillian smiled at him suddenly. 'You never did get over watching Columbo on television, did you, Peter?'

'You know him?' said Tom.

'We were at school together,' said Gillian.

'Of course you were,' said Tom. 'Everyone knows everyone in this town.'

Penny looked thoughtfully at Godwin. 'Shouldn't you be off duty at this time of night?'

Godwin looked at her pointedly. 'Not when there's still so much going on.'

'The streets looked deserted to me,' I said.

'They are,' said Godwin. 'Most of the town is properly concerned at the thought of a murderer still running around loose. And yet somehow I keep bumping into people.'

120

'What do you want with us?' said Robert.

'There's still no evidence to indicate why the Reverend Allen was murdered,' said Godwin. 'I need to know more about the man. Did any of you know him well?'

Gillian and Tom looked at each other, and then at Robert, and all three of them shrugged pretty much simultaneously.

'We only met him when we came to town for the wedding,' said Gillian.

'And we only talked to him a few times,' said Tom.

'He seemed pleasant enough,' said Gillian.

'Oh yes, very pleasant,' said Tom.

'What did you talk about?' said Godwin.

'The wedding, of course!' said Gillian.

'Gillian has very specific ideas about what she wants, and doesn't want, in the ceremony,' said Tom.

'Did you and the Reverend Allen disagree?' said Godwin. 'Were there any arguments?'

'Of course not,' said Gillian. 'He was happy to go along with whatever changes I suggested.'

'People do tend to do that,' said Tom. 'Once Gillian has put her mind to something.'

'Hush, darling,' said Gillian.

'Yes dear,' said Tom.

'Did you talk about anything else?' said Godwin, concentrating on Tom.

'Not really,' said Tom. 'He was very business-like; and very busy.'

'Weren't you concerned, when he didn't turn up for the wedding rehearsal at the church hall?'

'We had no reason to worry,' said Gillian. 'We just thought he was running late.'

'Because he was so busy,' said Tom.

'Exactly,' said Gillian.

'Who else was with you?' said Godwin.

'Really, Peter?' said Gillian. 'You want to go through all of this again?'

'Just answer the question, please,' said Godwin.

'The two of us,' said Tom, with heavy patience. 'Along with the best man, the bridesmaid; and Robert, of course.'

'Did any of you leave the church hall at any time, before the vicar's body was discovered?'

Gillian shrugged angrily. 'We all came and went, I suppose. We all had things to do. There's a lot of work involved, with putting on a wedding. We weren't keeping an eye on each other. Why would we?'

'So really, none of you have an alibi,' said Godwin.

'Do we need one?' said Tom.

'I don't know,' said Godwin. 'Do you?'

'We were all in the church hall together when the church bell started ringing,' Robert said firmly.

'But not before that,' said Godwin. 'How well did you know the Reverend Allen, Mr Bergin?'

'Not well,' said Robert, holding onto his patience with both hands. 'He hadn't been here long. Barely two years, which is nothing in a town like this. He didn't push himself on people. He restricted his preaching to the pulpit.' He gave Godwin a hard look. 'You've asked all of this before. Do we really need to go through it again?'

'It's important to check these things,' said Godwin. 'To get the details right.'

'Then why aren't you making notes?' said Robert.

'Will the rest of the police be back by tomorrow?' said Tom, just a bit pointedly.

'It doesn't seem likely,' Godwin said reluctantly. 'Apparently the industrial accident is still out of control. They'll be here as soon as they can.'

'What accident is this, exactly?' I said.

'There's been a major fire at a chemical plant,' said Godwin. 'A lot of people have been badly injured. Containing the fire, and evacuating the surrounding area, is proving a bigger problem than anyone anticipated.' He turned back to Gillian and Tom. 'If you don't feel safe going through with the wedding, my advice would be to call it off.'

'You'll be there to protect us, won't you?' said Gillian.

'I'll be around,' said Godwin. 'I wasn't sent an invitation, even though we were friends at school.'

Gillian smiled. 'A bit more than friends, for a while.'

Godwin smiled then, in spite of himself. 'That was a long time ago.'

'That was yesterday,' said Gillian.

Tom looked like he wanted to say something, but had enough sense not to.

'I would have sent you an invitation, Peter, if I'd known you were still in the area,' said Gillian. 'But you always said you wanted to be a big city cop.'

'Things don't always work out the way we plan,' said Godwin.

'Well, you're invited now,' said Gillian. 'You'll be very welcome. Isn't that right, Tom?'

'Oh yes,' said Tom. 'Absolutely.'

'I will do whatever it takes, to make sure you're safe,' said Godwin.

And perhaps I was the only one who noticed that he was only looking at Gillian when he said that.

'Of course you will,' said Gillian.

Godwin nodded briskly, and assumed his professional air again. 'I have to ask: are there perhaps any ex-boyfriends or ex-girlfriends with bad feelings? Anyone who might want to sabotage the wedding?'

'No,' said Gillian.

'This isn't the legend,' Tom said curtly. 'There's no spurned witch with a butcher's knife lurking in the background. The curse is just a story. You should know that, Inspector.'

Godwin merely nodded in response, before turning to Robert. 'If I could just ask you a few last questions, Mr Bergin. About your background.'

'I was in the civil service,' said Robert, with what I thought was an admirably straight face.

'That can cover a lot of ground,' said Godwin. 'You seem to have surprisingly important connections, Mr Bergin. Because the moment I started asking questions about you, my superiors shut me down. In fact, it was made very clear to me that you were to be left strictly alone.'

'Then they must have their reasons, mustn't they?' said Robert.

'What reasons might those be, Mr Bergin?'

'Ask your superiors.'

Godwin turned to Penny.

'I am independently wealthy,' she said happily.

'Is that all?' said Godwin.

'Isn't that enough?' said Penny.

Godwin turned to me. 'And what about you?'

'He's mine,' said Penny.

I nodded solemnly. Godwin gave up on us as a bad job, and turned back to Gillian.

'Are you really determined to go ahead with the wedding as planned? Despite everything that's happened?'

'Of course,' said Gillian. 'We've got guests arriving tomorrow from all over the country. This is going to be the biggest wedding Bradenford has ever seen.'

'And there's nothing you or anyone else can do to stop it,' said Tom.

Godwin gave him a sour look. 'If it was up to me the whole church would be sealed off and preserved as a crime scene.'

'Then it's just as well it's not up to you then, isn't it?' said Robert.

'Don't depend on your connections too much, Mr Bergin. They won't protect you if I decide to haul you off to the local police station and interrogate you. I will do whatever I feel necessary to get to the bottom of this.'

'Don't you speak to my father like that, Peter!' said Gillian.

'I'm just doing my job,' said Godwin.

'I think it's time you went and did it somewhere else,' said Tom.

Godwin turned his back on all of us, and stalked out of the bar. Everyone relaxed a little, though Gillian was still fuming. She managed a smile for Tom.

'Sorry about that. He didn't use to be such a dick.'

'Well,' said Tom. 'He's here on his own, so he's obviously feeling the pressure. But he was a dick.'

Gillian laughed, and looked round at the rest of us. 'Tom and I are going up to our room. Hopefully to get some sleep before the big day tomorrow.'

'I know I'll feel a lot safer, once we're back in our room and behind a locked door,' said Tom.

'Are you going to jam a chair up against the door again?' said Penny.

'Damn right,' said Tom. 'I'd shove the wardrobe against it, if I thought I could shift it.'

'He's so protective,' said Gillian.

'We can get a taxi back to my place,' Robert said to me and Penny. 'Normally I'd walk. Good exercise. But the way things are . . .'

'We'll call a taxi,' I said.

Back in the lobby, Gillian hugged her father, Tom gave him a manly handshake, and then the two of them trudged up the stairs to the top floor. Because there wasn't an elevator. Robert asked Nettie to call a taxi, and she got straight on the phone. Robert and Penny and I moved off a

126

distance, so we could talk quietly. Nettie had very keen ears under that unfortunate wig.

'They should be safe enough in their room tonight,' I said.

Robert nodded quickly. 'There's nothing in any of the stories about the demon attacking anyone here. But then, it never killed a vicar in advance of the wedding before. I won't relax until those two are safely married, and past their wedding night. Even if I have to stand guard outside their door till morning.'

'I'm sure that will help put them in the mood,' said Penny.

Robert surprised us with a brief bark of laughter then, before slowly shaking his head. 'I'm not sure anyone in this town is safe. The only thing all the stories agree on is that the curse is cruel.'

'You really think the vicar was killed by an invisible demon?' I said.

'Don't you?' said Robert.

'I'm not convinced,' I said carefully. 'I haven't found any evidence.'

'Then you need to look harder!' said Robert. 'We're running out of time!'

He broke off as he realized his voice had risen enough to attract Nettie's attention. She peered at us anxiously from behind her desk.

'Is everything all right, dears?'

'Everything's fine,' I said. 'It's just late, and the day's problems are getting to us. But the wedding will take place tomorrow, as planned.'

'That's good to know, dear,' said Nettie. 'The whole town's been looking forward to it. And

I've invested quite a lot of money on getting just the right food for the buffet . . .'

Perhaps fortunately, we were interrupted as the front door crashed open and Cathy came striding in, grinning cheerfully. 'OK; who wants to get the hell out of here? Your magic and reasonably-priced chariot awaits!'

'Are you the only cab driver in this town?' said Penny.

'I'm the only one who's prepared to be out and about at this time of night,' said Cathy. 'All the other drivers called in sick, though they're not fooling anyone. You can't really blame them. Everyone in this town takes the Bergin family curse very seriously. That's what happens when cousins can't be bothered to get out of the gene pool to take a leak.'

'Has no one ever told you that constant cheerfulness can be very wearing?' I said.

'Oh yes . . .' said Cathy. 'Come on; I'll drive you out to the old dark Bergin house. And if the bogeyman shows up along the way, I'll run the bugger over.'

Outside, the taxi was the only vehicle parked in the street. The night was disturbingly quiet, and the harsh light from the street lamps made everything look artificial, like the setting for a low-budget horror movie. I just hoped the monster wouldn't amount to much. Penny moved in beside Cathy as we headed for the taxi.

'Since you know everyone and everything, can you tell us why Nettie wears such an obvious wig?'

128

'Chemotherapy,' said Cathy. 'She puts on a brave front, but word is it's not going well. Sorry you asked now, aren't you? That's small towns for you; all human life is here, the good and the bad. It doesn't help that Nettie has to run that dump pretty much single-handed. Or that her son's such a complete waste of space.'

'You weren't much better, at that age,' said Robert, as he manoeuvred himself carefully into the front seat.

'Are you kidding?' said Cathy. 'I was a real pain in the arse! But I like to think I had style.'

'That's one word for it,' said Robert.

Penny and I climbed into the back seat as Cathy slipped behind the wheel. She gave us just enough time to do up our seat belts, and then started the engine with a flourish.

'Atomic batteries to power, turbines to speed, and warp factor six, Mister Sulu!'

We shot off through the town, ignoring all speed restrictions and most of the traffic lights, whatever colour they were showing.

'One good thing about empty streets,' Cathy said loudly over her shoulder, 'You don't have to worry about any other traffic. I could even drive on the other side of the road if you like!'

'Please don't,' I said.

'So,' said Cathy. 'Have you been having fun, enjoying the town's night life?'

'I wasn't aware there was any,' said Penny, holding onto her seat belt with both hands.

'Mostly there isn't,' Cathy said airily. 'You have to go all the way to the next town if you want to scare up some real excitement. Though

129

I wouldn't recommend it. The kids are animals. They drink like someone's going to take it away, and if they don't start any trouble the bouncers will.'

'Have you seen anything unusual in town tonight?' I said.

'Not a thing,' said Cathy. 'The town is dead, if you'll pardon the expression. Of course, I spent most of the evening sitting in the taxi rank in the middle of town, with my new doctor and nurse romance novel. There's nothing like a starched uniform and surgical gloves to brighten up a furtive embrace. So, is the wedding still on?'

'Yes,' said Robert, staring straight ahead. Possibly because he was afraid to look away.

'The wedding should bring the town back to its senses,' said Cathy, tapping the brakes a few times, just for show. 'We do love a good wedding, especially if there's a television star involved. And Nettie always puts on a good spread afterwards.'

'Are you invited?' said Penny.

'Of course!' said Cathy. 'Old school friend, me. I taught Gilly her first rude word, and stole her first boyfriend. You don't forget bonds like that. I should have been her maid of honour, but I'm not respectable enough for a wedding as special as this. Right, Mr Bergin?' She laughed cheerfully when Robert didn't say anything. 'Hopefully once those two are safely hitched, and nothing bad has happened, the town will gather its collective marbles again and we can all get back to normal. Curses should stay in books, where they belong.'

* * *

I felt increasingly tense as we left the bright lights of the town behind, and headed out toward the open moorland. Robert's house wasn't far outside the town, but there was only a single street light at the beginning of the lane that led to it, so we were soon driving away from the light and into a gathering gloom. The taxi's headlights illuminated the road ahead, but that was all. And with no lights on inside Robert's house, it was just a dark shape against the night sky.

Cathy brought the taxi to a shuddering halt right outside the front door. The bright headlights splashed across the front of the house, as though indicating where safety lay. I was out the back of the taxi in a moment, with Penny right behind me, while Robert took his time heaving his old bones out of the front seat. I was careful to stay in the light, and kept a watchful eye on our surroundings. This looked like a really good place for an ambush. Robert carefully sorted out some money, and handed it over to Cathy. She looked at it, and then at him.

'You call that a tip? I've found more than this down the back of my sofa!'

'I'm a pensioner,' said Robert, entirely unmoved. 'I should qualify for a special discount.'

'Oh stop, please,' said Cathy. 'You're breaking my heart.'

She gave us all one last cheerful wave, swung the taxi round in a tight arc and roared off back to town, taking the light with her. Alone in the dark, the night was quiet as the grave. Robert headed straight for the front door, apparently not in the least bothered by the gloom. He thrust his key straight into the lock with the ease of long practice, pushed the door back, and fished around inside for the light switch. The hall light snapped on, and a reassuringly warm glow spilled out onto the path. Robert went inside, and I hurried in after him. Picking up on my mood, Penny was right behind me. Robert closed the front door and locked it, and then patted the heavy wood a few times. To make sure the door was shut, or to encourage it to do its job and keep the bad things out.

'Well,' I said to him. 'I promised you we'd find the time for a proper sit down and chat about the old days, and this would seem to be it.'

'No thanks, Ishmael,' said Robert. 'It's been a long day, and I'm tired.'

He didn't say it out loud, but I got the impression he felt he'd said all he needed to back at The Swan. He smiled briefly as he realized it was my turn to be disappointed.

'We'll talk more tomorrow,' he said gruffly. 'You two go on up. I'll turn in once I've checked everything is locked up safely. You can't be too careful.'

He moved off into the house, and I looked around for the switch that turned on the light for the stairs. Even then, it took me a moment before I was ready to start up the narrow wooden steps. Penny moved in close beside me.

'Ishmael? What is it? What's wrong?'

'Too many things to talk about, this late in the evening,' I said, smiling back at her reassuringly. 'You look almost as tired as I feel. Let's just get some sleep. It's going to be a long day tomorrow, with lots to do before the wedding.'

'You know I can always tell when you're keeping something from me,' said Penny.

'I know,' I said. 'But I'm tired. Let's talk about it tomorrow.'

Some time later I lay in bed in the dark, with Penny sleeping beside me. It was only a single bed, but there was just enough room as long as we snuggled together. Penny made soft snuffling sounds as she slept. Normally I find that a comforting sound, when I wake in the night, but now it just made Penny seem more vulnerable. More in need of protecting. And I wasn't sure I could do that any more.

I was tired, but I had no intention of sleeping. I was afraid to sleep in case the dream came back. In case my old self tried to break free. I felt like I was losing control; of myself, and my life. I was scared I might close my eyes and wake up as someone, or something, else. Like Jekyll giving way to Hyde, or a werewolf bursting out of its human host. In my mind's eye I saw my human shape melt and twist, becoming something horrible as my humanity was over-written by a monstrous memory.

Or perhaps I'd still look human, but an entirely different mind would look out at the world through my eyes, and see the woman sleeping beside him as the real monster.

I wondered if I'd ever dare sleep again. Though I couldn't even be sure of hanging onto myself while I was awake, not after what happened earlier tonight; when for a moment I'd felt alien breath on the back of my neck. If this continued I'd have no choice but to leave Penny. To get as far away from her as possible, to make sure my other self couldn't hurt her. Leave Penny and the Organization and the life I'd made for myself far behind, and head for somewhere remote and isolated. So I couldn't hurt anyone.

I didn't want to go. The time Penny and I had spent together was the happiest I'd ever known. But now it seemed that was coming to an end. After all these years without aging, I was dying. Because the alien couldn't return without completely erasing me. I fought back the sudden rush of despair with concentrated anger and defiance. I'd spent so many years fighting to live life on my own terms. I wasn't about to give up now.

I would fight to be Ishmael, to be human. Fight with everything I had, to stay in control long enough to see Gillian and Tom safely married, and make sure they survived the night after. My wedding gift to the young couple; and a long-delayed thank you to Robert, for the warning that allowed me to get away from Black Heir just in time.

And, perhaps, for not escorting me to Hazard Asylum.

I lay awake in the dark, seeing every detail of the room perfectly clearly, over and over again. I could hear Robert snoring, in his room down the corridor. Penny snuggled up against me and murmured something in her sleep, but didn't wake. And I promised her, silently, that I would die before I let her come to any harm. I would kill the monster in me before I let it hurt her. Even if it meant killing me.

I lay awake in the dark, forcing back the tiredness minute by minute, hour by hour, all through the long and endless night.

Seven
Enemy Action

Even the longest night draws finally to a close.

The next morning, after a surprisingly healthy breakfast of All-Bran and fruit juices, Robert and Penny and I left the house and walked back into town. Given how tired I was, I would much rather have taken a taxi; even if it was driven by Cathy. But Robert insisted that since it was a lovely sunny morning, a stretch of the legs would do us all good. I wasn't convinced, but if Robert could contemplate walking all the way into town at his age I didn't see how I could reasonably object.

At first, I didn't so much walk as stumble. After a night without any rest, because I didn't dare relax my self-control for a moment, I was exhausted. I'd barely managed three words over breakfast, and it hadn't gone unnoticed. But the bright sunlight and the fresh morning air helped to sweep the cobwebs out of my thoughts, and soon enough Penny and I were strolling along behind Robert as he strode down the narrow lane humming what he fondly imagined was a tune.

The lane was bordered on both sides by low drystone walls and great open fields, with grass so green it was practically fluorescent. The sky

was a deep blue, with clouds drifting purpose-
fully past overhead as though they were late for
an appointment. It was still unnaturally quiet,
without even a hint of birdsong. As though they
were hiding, afraid to draw attention to themselves. Penny punched my arm lightly, to get
my attention.

'You look awful. There are dark smudges under
your eyes, you've barely done anything but grunt
at me since you got up, and you're walking like
something inside you is broken. Did you get any
sleep at all last night?'

'Not much,' I said.

'You should have said something. We could
have sat up and talked for a while.'

'You needed your sleep,' I said.

Penny gave me a hard look. The one that
meant: *You're the one who needs looking after,
not me*. She knew something was wrong, but she
couldn't tell what. She slipped her arm through
mine anyway, to show I was forgiven, and we
walked on down the lane.

Robert strode ahead of us as though he was
leading a parade, though he was already getting
short of breath. I wanted to tell him to pace
himself but I knew he wouldn't listen. He was
trying to convince himself he was still the same
man he used to be, the last time we were together;
and who was I to tell him different? I looked
about me, drinking in the morning. The town
was actually a lot closer than it had seemed last
night, when the lane was full of darkness.
Already I could hear traffic roaring through the
streets, and the bustle of a town waking up and

setting about its business. Penny felt me relax, and pressed my arm against her side.

'Best foot forward, Ishmael. We have a murderer to catch.'

'I'll keep an eye out for him,' I said. 'Unless he's invisible, of course. You know what these demons are like.'

'I could go and walk with Robert, you know.'

Once we'd entered the town, and Robert had reluctantly slowed to an amble, Bradenford seemed very different from the night before. People were out and about everywhere, bustling up and down the old narrow streets and nodding and smiling to each other. The roads were crammed with cars and vans, buses and coaches. Apparently the town was only scared while it was dark. And yet, even though most of the people we passed acknowledged Robert with a smile or a nod, and sometimes a brief cheerful comment about the wedding, no one wanted to stop and chat. They just hurried along, as though determined to be finished with their business while the sun was still in the sky. So they could rush home, lock their doors, and feel safe.

Penny and I got quite a few suspicious looks simply because we weren't local. Strangers weren't to be trusted with a killer on the loose. Penny and I made a point of smiling cheerfully at everyone, but it didn't make any difference. The traffic grew heavier as we entered the town centre, but I couldn't help noticing that the drivers and passengers were all staring straight ahead, ignoring their surroundings. Perhaps in the hope the town would overlook them.

Robert finally brought us to the church hall, at the far end of the same street as Trinity Church. Robert stopped before the heavy wooden door and then just stood there for a moment, getting his breath back. From the sounds he was making that was going to take a while, so Penny and I tactfully turned away to study the church hall. It was another old building, with rough stone walls, shuttered windows and a gabled roof in clear need of repair. A brass plaque on the wall proudly announced that the church hall dated back to the fifteenth century. Robert stretched his back till it creaked, and then pushed the door open and led the way in.

The interior was one great open space, with bright sunlight pouring in through the wide windows. Judging by the colourful posters tacked on the walls, the hall was home to a great many local groups. Everything from local dramatic productions to cookery groups, flower-arranging classes and organized walks for charity. Penny studied the posters and then turned to me.

'Cathy was right; if you're looking for excitement you're not going to find it here in town.'

'I doubt the local swingers groups or black magic covens advertise for new members in a setting like this,' I said.

'You honestly think they have such things here?' said Penny.

'Big cities are nothing compared to small towns, when it comes to the more exotic forms of sinning,' I said.

'Do you suppose groups like that could have something to do with . . .'

'No,' I said firmly. 'What's happening here is a new thing. That's why everyone is so frightened of it.'

'Just asking,' said Penny.

We looked down to the end of the long room, where Gillian and Tom were having quiet but determined words with a middle-aged man in a nice suit and a vicar's dog collar. Tom was wearing a stylish grey morning suit, complete with top hat and gloves. He carried it off well; probably because as an actor he was used to making costumes look like clothes. Gillian was wearing a marvellous ivory white off-the-shoulder wedding dress, with the veil pushed well back so she could concentrate on intimidating the vicar. Penny shook her head, frowning.

'She shouldn't be wearing that. The groom isn't supposed to see the bride in her dress before the ceremony. It's all kinds of bad luck.'

'I told her that,' Robert said gruffly. 'But Gillian won't be told, once she's put her mind to something.'

I looked across at the two other people present; David the best man, in another morning suit, and a young woman in a fluffy pink bridesmaid's outfit. They were watching Gillian and Tom ganging up on the vicar with the look of people who were glad they weren't involved. I drew Robert's attention to them, and he nodded quickly.

'That's David Barnes, the best man; and Karen

140

Nicholls the bridesmaid. I'll leave it to you to work out which is which.'

'Who's the new vicar?' I said.

'The Reverend Stewart, from Limply Stoke,' said Robert.

'That's never the name of a real town!' said Penny.

'It's traditional,' said Robert. 'And probably meant something quite innocent at the time.'

'Like what?' challenged Penny.

'Don't press me,' said Robert. 'The origins of a lot of town names are lost in history, and legend. And there's no denying people could have an odd sense of humour, back in the day.'

I let the two of them get on with it, while I concentrated my hearing on what the happy couple were saying to the vicar. It seemed Gillian was being very particular about changes she wanted made to the wedding vows; very definitely including no mention of *honour and obey*. There seemed no end to the alterations she wanted, which made me wonder why she didn't just write her own vows and be done with it. The vicar kept saying, 'But it's traditional . . .' and getting nowhere. Every now and again he would look hopefully at Tom, but there was no help to be found in that quarter.

'I've spent years planning how my wedding should go,' Gillian said remorselessly. 'Right down to the tiniest detail. This is going to be the happiest day of my life and if it isn't someone is going to suffer for it.'

'Trust me,' Tom said easily to the vicar. 'She means it. She'd made up her mind what she wanted on her wedding day long before she met me.'

'It's my wedding,' said Gillian.

Tom looked like he wanted to say, *Actually, it's our wedding* . . . but he had enough sense not to. There's a time and a place for being right. He settled for giving the vicar a commiserating look, as if to say, *Don't waste your breath.*

The best man and the bridesmaid finally noticed us, and come down the hall to make themselves known. There was a brief outbreak of smiles and hand-shaking as we all introduced ourselves. Gillian and Tom didn't even look round. David wore his morning suit as though it was just something he'd thrown on that morning.

'It's a splendid outfit, isn't it?' he said cheerfully. 'I suppose it appeals to my theatrical nature. If you're going to make a first impression, go big, that's what I always say.'

Just standing there he positively burned with charisma, as though he was the star and we were all just bit players.

'Tom and I have been knocking around together for years,' he said cheerfully.

'Where did you and Tom first meet?' said Penny. Because women always want to know things like that.

'At drama school,' David said easily. 'Best mates from the start. We found out we worked well together, and we've hardly been apart since. Appearing in the same shows, on stage and on television. Usually as hero and villain, though we often have to flip a coin as to who's going

142

to read for which. I mostly prefer the villain; because they get all the best lines.'

'And Tom?' said Penny.

'Oh, he adores playing the hero,' said David. 'More action, and he always gets the girl. And he does so love to be loved by the audience. Sorry, I'm being waspish, aren't I? And on his wedding day, of all days. That's what years in the theatre does to you. Still, we're often requested as a package by agents and producers. Like Cushing and Lee, in the old Hammer horror movies.'

'I don't like horror movies,' said Karen Nicholls, seizing a chance to get a word in when David paused for breath. 'I don't know why people want to be frightened; isn't the world a scary enough place as it is?'

Karen was short, well-padded, in her late twenties, and clearly only wearing her fluffy pink outfit under protest. She had dark curly hair, emphatic make-up, and frightened eyes. She kept trying to smile but it never lasted long; as though dark thoughts kept interrupting it. She looked down at her dress, and shrugged resignedly.

'I know . . . It's really not me. But what Gillian wants, Gillian gets. I should know; we've been best friends for ages. Ever since we both started out as political researchers. Which is all I ever wanted; Gillian is the ambitious one.'

'What does she want to be?' said Penny. 'Eventually?'

'Prime Minister, probably,' said Karen, managing a genuine smile for the first time. 'Or possibly Queen.' And then the smile disappeared as she fixed me with a worried look. Like someone wondering whether the light at the end of the tunnel might turn out to be an oncoming train. 'Gillian said you're here to protect us. I'm glad someone is, but . . . what do you think, about the Bergin curse? Gillian never said a word about it until I got here. And then the vicar died . . . That poor man.'

'Gillian never mentioned the curse before, even though she's been talking about the marriage for years?' I said.

'Not a single word,' said Karen. 'And now I know why. It's such a creepy story. After what happened to the Reverend Allen I expected the wedding to be called off, but I should have known better. Even though it's not respectful. Not right . . . I mean, the murderer's still out there somewhere! He could come after any of us! I didn't dare leave my hotel room until it was light. I don't feel safe, even now.'

'You're in a church hall, surrounded by people,' said David. 'You couldn't be safer if you were wearing pink Kevlar. The vicar's death was just an unfortunate coincidence, that's all.' He looked over to where Gillian and Tom were taking it in turns to browbeat the Reverend Stewart. David sighed heavily, and just a bit theatrically. 'This is clearly going to take some time, so we might as well make ourselves comfortable. Gillian doesn't look like she's willing to settle for anything less than complete capitulation, and I wouldn't be the one to bet against her.'

'She gets it from her mother,' said Robert, and we all turned to look at him for a moment.

'There's got to be some chairs around here somewhere,' said David, looking up and down the empty room. 'How can you have a church hall, and no chairs?'

'How did the Reverend Allen react to all these changes in the ceremony?' I said, before he could go wandering off.

'He never turned up to discuss them,' said David. 'But he seemed . . . easy-going enough.'

He looked to Karen for confirmation, and she nodded quickly.

'Oh yes. He was very nice. Very . . .'

'Pleasant?' said Penny.

Karen beamed at her. 'Yes! That's the word. I liked him . . .' And then she remembered, and her smile disappeared like a blown-out candle. I thought she might shed a few tears, but in the end she remembered her mascara, and didn't.

'Look on the bright side,' David said cheerfully. 'At least we're not the ones getting married, which means we're not the main targets. If the killer should turn up at the wedding, like in the old story, we'll just have to use the happy couple as human shields.'

We all managed some kind of smile. Karen actually giggled, and seemed to relax a little.

'Gillian was going on about the kind of marriage she wanted even before she and Tom were officially engaged,' she said. 'She's been obsessed with having the perfect day for as long as I can remember.'

'Why does it mean so much to her?' said Penny.

'She's never said, but . . .' Karen glanced at Gillian to make sure she wasn't listening, and then lowered her voice anyway. 'I sometimes wonder if it's because deep down, she never really believed it would happen. She's such a . . . strong personality, she was always breaking up with boyfriends. Gillian's not the easiest of people to get on with . . . I mean, if you're a man. She and I have always got on fine. Probably because I'm not any competition for her. But I have to say . . . I've never seen her so happy with anyone as she is with Tom.'

'And how does Tom feel, about all this perfectionism?' I said.

'He wants Gillian to have whatever she wants,' said Karen. 'Isn't that just so romantic?'

'He's always been a pushover where women are concerned,' David said amiably. 'But then, he's always taken direction well.'

'Excuse me,' said Robert, with the air of someone who'd been left out of the conversation for far too long. 'I think I'll go and check out the side room; make sure the wedding cake was delivered there, as promised. If it hasn't been, or if it's not everything Gillian asked for, there's going to be trouble. Because there's not much time left to put things right.'

I glanced at the big clock on the wall; 10.25. And the wedding was scheduled for 2.00 p.m. So all I had to do was keep everyone alive for a few more hours. If only I could be sure what I was protecting them from . . . While I was thinking about that, Robert disappeared through the only other door in the room, closing it firmly behind him. He knew it wasn't wise to go off on his own, but this was his way of saying that

146

he could still take care of business, and look after himself.

'Now he's gone,' said David, 'And I don't have to worry about being on the receiving end of one of Mr Bergin's famous disapproving looks, maybe we can finally have a proper conversation about the Bergin family curse. I just love all the gory details! I started looking into it after Tom told me about the legendary curse that came along with his bride. Did you know the original couple were actually hacked to pieces, right in front of the altar? And after the witch was hanged, they tore out her heart and burnt it separately!'

'That's horrible!' said Karen.

'I think that's the point,' said David.

'I don't believe the original couple were hacked apart,' I said.

David bristled at being challenged on his favourite subject. 'How can you be so sure about that? She had every reason! And a butcher's knife!'

'But all the accounts agree that the murders took place in front of the gathered family and friends,' I said. 'She'd only have had time to get in a few good blows, before she would have been overpowered and dragged away. The burning of the heart is more likely; that was a traditional method of dealing with witches. To make sure they wouldn't rise from their grave to trouble the living.'

'But it didn't work,' said Karen. Her mouth tightened into a flat line, and her voice was a small scared thing. 'She might not have returned, but her demonic familiar did. The curse lives on.'

'You don't have anything to worry about,' Penny said soothingly. 'Robert brought Ishmael and me in specially to look out for everyone's safety.'

'You're bodyguards?' said David, looking at us with new interest.

'Sometimes,' I said.

Karen shook her head, refusing to be comforted. 'I have a bad feeling about all of this. I did from the first moment I arrived here. This town just . . . feels wrong. Like it's haunted by the past. Or possessed by it.'

'The curse is just an old story,' David said firmly. 'Like Bluebeard, or Little Red Riding Hood. Cautionary tales to encourage safe and proper behaviour in the young. You might as well worry that the church is going to be blown down by the Big Bad Wolf.'

He laughed easily, and Karen managed a smile. I didn't say anything; but I couldn't help remembering the old stories of werewolves attacking the town. Karen looked David over approvingly.

'You look like you could handle any trouble that might come our way. You do know the best man has certain duties and privileges, where the bridesmaid is concerned?'

'Ah, sorry,' said David. 'I'm afraid that's not going to happen. I bat for the other team.'

Karen shot him a disgusted look. 'Actors!'

'Not all of them,' said Gillian.

She came striding down the room to join us,

dragging Tom along by the hand. He seemed happy enough to be dragged. Their worries from the evening before had apparently been dismissed by the bright sunshine, and their rapidly approaching wedding. They came to a halt before us, and struck a pose so we could admire their outfits.

'Doesn't she look marvellous?' Tom said proudly.

'Amazing!' David said cheerfully.

'Just like the design you showed me, all those years ago,' said Karen.

Penny did her best not to frown, but I could see the effort it took.

'I thought it was bad luck for the groom to see the bride in her dress before the wedding?' she said politely.

'Oh, I can't be bothered with things like that,' Gillian said immediately. 'I've far too much work to do; and getting in and out of this dress is a real pain. Tom had to send out for a shoehorn. Besides, he absolutely refuses to let me out of his sight for a moment, until we're safely married.'

Tom smiled and shrugged, looking pressured and proud at the same time.

The Reverend Stewart hurried past us, smiling nervously as he headed for the exit. Clearly hoping to make his escape before Gillian could think of something else to argue about. But in the end he paused anyway, because he felt he should say something. If only to make it clear he wasn't running away.

'I'm just popping up to the church, to make

sure everything is ready for the service this afternoon,' he said, doing his best to smile at all of us at once.

'You aren't bothered by the fact that your predecessor was murdered there?' I said bluntly.

His back straightened immediately, his head came up, and he made a point of meeting my gaze steadily. The smile was gone.

'I'm doing this especially for poor Franklin. He was a good man, who deserved a better end than being strung up in his own church as a sick joke. I will perform the ceremony in his honour; because that's what he would have wanted me to do.'

He nodded sharply, and left the hall. Tom looked after him.

'If he'd shown that much backbone during our discussions, we'd probably still be arguing.'

'I think he only works up a sweat for things that matter,' I said.

I glanced at Gillian to see how she would react to that, but she just shrugged. 'I had him eating out of my hand by the end. Everything's arranged, down to the last detail. Now, Tom and I have to be going. I just had a call to say the last of our guests have arrived at The Swan.'

'Nettie has opened the bar specially, just for them,' said Tom. 'At special prices, no doubt.'

'I think we need to go back and take quick look, to make sure they're being treated properly,' said Gillian.

'Before you go,' I said, 'can I just ask, how did you persuade the Reverend Stewart to come and help out, at such short notice?'

'We didn't,' said Gillian. 'Dad took care of all that.'

'And according to Robert, the Reverend Stewart volunteered,' said Tom. 'No argument at all. Said it was his duty, and the danger just made it a test of his faith. Though I think he's starting to see Gillian as the real test of his faith.'

'I think it's very brave of him,' Gillian said firmly. 'Though he should be safe enough. The Reverend Allen was killed at night, when he was on his own; the Reverend Stewart will be marrying us in broad daylight, in front of the entire congregation.'

'You really think that's going to make a difference?' said David.

'There's nothing in any of the stories about anyone being killed during the day,' Gillian insisted, her voice rising.

'There was nothing in the stories about a vicar being killed, until it happened,' David said reasonably. 'I know, I've read all the books.'

'Even the really trashy ones,' said Tom.

David grinned. 'I liked those best.'

While they were all busy scoring points off each other, Penny moved in close beside me and lowered her voice. 'Why are you so interested in the Reverend Stewart?'

'Think about it,' I said, just as quietly. 'Who will be closest to the happy couple, with the best chance of getting to them? Maybe Allen was killed just so Stewart could replace him . . .'

'You really don't trust anyone, do you?' said Penny.

'No,' I said. 'Apart from you, of course.'

151

'Nice save,' Penny said sweetly.

'Hey!' Gillian said suddenly. 'Where's Dad?'

I looked around quickly, but before any of us could say anything, the side door burst open and Robert appeared, pushing a wheeled trolley ahead of him. On which was balanced, somewhat precariously, a multi-tiered wedding cake with white icing, pink ruffles, and a soft gooey top with two figures to represent the bride and groom. They looked to me like they were standing knee deep in snow, but I didn't say anything. The figures were wearing the exact same outfits as Gillian and Tom. Robert brought the trolley to a halt right in front of us, and we all gathered around the cake, making appropriate appreciative noises.

'Gillian designed her own cake too,' Tom said proudly.

'I sent the baker advance photos of our outfits,' said Gillian. 'To make sure he'd get the figures exactly right.'

'Is everything as it should be?' said Robert. 'Or do I need to make a phone call and really ruin the baker's day?'

There was a tense pause as Gillian studied the cake intently, and we all relaxed a little when she nodded briskly.

'He's done a good job,' she said.

'Oh good,' said Tom.

'And if he hadn't?' said David.

'Then I would have been very upset,' said Gillian.

'And no one wants that,' Tom said smoothly.

'Aren't you in charge of anything about this wedding?' said David.

152

'This is Gillian's day,' said Tom. 'And I don't want a single thing to go wrong with any of it.'

'Isn't he wonderful?' said Gillian.

They smiled fondly at each other, and for a moment it was as though there wasn't anyone else in the room.

'Has everyone had a good look at the cake?' said Robert. 'Fine. I'll wheel it back into the side room, so it can be wheeled out for the reception.'

He turned the trolley around and headed back to the side door.

'You're holding the reception here?' said Penny. 'I thought Nettie was in charge of all that?'

'She's only providing the food,' said Gillian. 'She did offer us The Swan's function room, but it really wasn't big enough. Hell, this hall is only just big enough.'

'You did invite a hell of a lot of people,' said Tom. 'Not that I'm complaining . . .'

'What good is a perfect day, unless everyone is there to see it?' said Gillian.

'Of course,' said Tom.

'I'll be glad when this wedding is over,' said Karen. 'You know I want you to be happy on your big day, Gillian; but I won't feel safe till you've both said "I do" . . .'

'Pull yourself together, girl!' said Gillian. She put her arm around Karen, and hugged her encouragingly. 'Nothing bad is going to happen! Everything is going to work out fine, I promise you.'

'How can you be sure?' said Karen.

'Because I grew up with the Bergin curse,' said Gillian. 'So I know it's nothing but a story.'

'I'm not sure the town would agree with you,' said David. 'Did you see how empty the streets were last night?'

'Just one of the many reasons I left this superstitious backwards-looking hole the first chance I got,' said Gillian.

She let go of Karen, and moved back to Tom.

'I don't understand why people only associated with the wedding are in danger,' said Karen.

She meant *why her*, though she didn't say it. David put an arm around her shoulders to steady her, and she looked at him thankfully. Gillian made an effort to be reassuring, as she saw her friend was genuinely frightened.

'If you take the old story seriously, then you have nothing to fear from the curse, Karen. It only threatens the bride and groom. There's nothing in it about bridesmaids. Tom and I are getting married in just a few hours. If we can be brave, so can you.'

Karen shook her head. 'You've always been brave. You think it's easy. And Tom will do anything you tell him.'

'Whether it's in his best interests or not,' said David.

Gillian smiled at Tom. 'I think that's what I like best about him.'

'Come on, Tom, show a little backbone!' said David. 'Stand up for yourself! Argue with her about something; even if it's only the hideous bow tie that came with the morning suits.'

Tom tried to look down at his bow tie, realized

he couldn't, and looked at David's. 'What's wrong with it?'

'Apart from the fact *it's a bow tie,* it's ugly and tasteless and the exact same colour as a baboon's arse!'

'I don't think I'm going to listen to you about style, after some of the things you've worn,' said Tom. 'Remember that naval outfit they put you in, for our last London show? We couldn't get you out of it for two weeks after the show finished!'

'It suited me,' David said loftily.

Karen turned suddenly to look at me. 'Do you believe in the Bergin curse?'

'I haven't uncovered any reason to believe it's operating here,' I said carefully. I looked around the group. 'I think it's far more likely someone is using the curse as a cover, to disguise their true intentions. Do any of you know anyone who might want to stop the wedding, through intimidation?'

'Why would anyone want to do that?' said David.

'Right!' said Tom. He was trying to sound angry at the very idea, but it came out more genuinely puzzled.

'Is there any money involved?' said Penny. 'Most murders are based around someone profiting. Does anyone stand to make or lose money, according to whether the marriage goes ahead?'

'I don't see how,' said Tom, frowning. 'There's no inheritance involved, no insurance money . . . I make decent money as an actor, but only when I'm working. There are long periods when I'm not.'

David nodded quickly in agreement. 'I've known Tom for ages. He's never had any real money, and he's never been known to give a damn about it. One of his more attractive qualities.'

'I'm just a researcher,' said Gillian. 'And Dad's retired. Whatever's going on, it's not about money.' She stopped, and looked steadily at Tom. 'You know I wouldn't go ahead with the wedding, if I thought you were in any real danger.'

'Of course you wouldn't,' said Tom. 'But no one's in any danger! Once the wedding is over and nothing bad has happened, everyone will see the curse is just an old legend and calm the hell down. So stop worrying, everyone.'

'Of course, we've still got to make it through the wedding night,' said Gillian.

'OK,' said Tom. 'No pressure . . .'

'If we're talking about the curse,' said David, his enthusiasm surfacing again, 'Gillian, can you tell us anything that isn't in the books? Any nasty little details that only a member of the Bergin family would know?'

Gillian was already shaking her head. 'There was a big breakup in the family, back in the nineteenth century. All the family money was lost in some really stupid business deal, and whole sections of the family stopped talking to each other. If anyone knew anything, those details are long gone. All I know about the curse is what I read in the books Dad had about the house. I went through them all, growing up, and that's how I know it's bullshit, because you can't find two books that agree on anything.'

She broke off as Robert emerged from the

side room. He looked surprised to see us all there.

'Why are you still standing around? Get a move on! There's lots to do before the wedding! I'm off to the church, to check everything's all right with the vicar, and make sure all the flowers have been delivered, as promised.'

'Tom and I are going back to The Swan,' said Gillian. 'Make sure our guests are being treated right.'

'I think I'll find a nice little tea shoppe,' said David, 'And run through my best man's speech again.'

'You're not still re-writing that thing, are you?' said Tom. 'How many ways are there to say, "I hope you'll both be very happy together"?'

'You'd be surprised,' David said darkly. 'According to this book I reason how to write a best man's speech, I'm supposed to provide amusing anecdotes to illuminate the groom's past and character. Don't worry, I won't mention Deirdre Turner.'

'Oh good,' said Tom. 'I'm so pleased you didn't bring her up.'

'Bring her up?' said David. 'Have you seen her recently? I couldn't lift her off her feet with a block and tackle.'

'Moving on,' said Tom, determinedly.

'Can I go with you, Gillian?' said Karen. 'I'm sure I could find something useful to do to help.'

Gillian nodded immediately, and Tom smiled at Karen reassuringly.

'Of course,' he said. 'Always lots to do. You just stick with us.'

'I think Penny and I will go visit the town library,' I said. 'Check out the local histories, for details on the original events.'

'I thought you didn't believe in the curse?' said Tom.

'It's possible someone else does,' I said. 'And if they do, I want to know everything they know.'

Robert provided us with directions. The library wasn't far, but then nothing was in this town. And so we all left the church hall, and went about our business.

Penny and I walked through streets teeming with people, none of whom wanted anything to do with us. There was a general sense of urgency, and up close the smiles seemed forced. I felt the hackles rise on the back of my neck, as I realized these people were genuinely scared. Penny and I pressed on through the streets, and found the library easily enough, but it turned out to be a wasted journey. All the old historical records had been destroyed in a fire at the previous library building, years ago. The only surviving accounts were in the local paper's archives. And just like that, Penny and I were back out on the street again.

'The trouble with this curse,' said Penny, 'is that there's nothing solid to get hold of.'

'Maybe that's the point,' I said. 'Whoever's behind this can hide anything in the mists of the past.'

'But who?' said Penny. 'And why?'

'Well that's the point, isn't it?' I said.

At which point we were ambushed by the

reporter Linda and her cameraman Ian. They came running down the street and planted themselves right in front of us, and with our backs pressed up against the library wall there was nowhere for us to run. Short of knocking them both down and trampling right over them; and I was tempted. Linda smiled at me engagingly, but I raised a hand to stop her before she could say anything.

'We've already told you everything we can.'

'There must be something else!' said Linda, just a bit desperately. 'You've got to help me out! The editor used absolutely everything I submitted to fill this morning's edition, and now he wants more! He's sent every warm body on the paper's payroll out onto the streets to browbeat people, so I have to come up with something special if I want to hang on to my byline.'

'Why not just cover the wedding?' said Penny. 'You said the editor wanted lots of photos.'

Linda pouted sulkily. 'I've been banned. Mr Bergin saw what I wrote, and didn't approve. He phoned the editor!'

'I'm out too,' said Ian. 'Just because I'm with her.'

Linda ignored him, fixing me with an imploring gaze. 'Mr Bergin said I was being too intrusive, but it wasn't personal! I think it's because I mostly wrote about the curse, and not his daughter's wedding.'

'I don't know why I got blamed along with you,' said Ian. 'Except that I always do. I'll just have to lurk around outside the church and grab

159

as many photos as I can when the happy couple emerge, before someone chases me off.'

Linda saw she wasn't getting anywhere being pleasant, and changed tactics. She took a step back and glowered at me suspiciously.

'What were you doing in the library?'

'No comment,' I said.

I gave Ian a hard look as he tried to sneak a photo of me, and he almost dropped his camera. Linda glared at him, and he shrugged helplessly.

'What can I do? He's bigger than me.'

'Everyone is,' she said sharply. 'How are you going to make a career in journalism, if you don't stand up for yourself?'

'I have you to do that for me,' said Ian. 'And you do it so well.'

Linda smiled. 'I do, don't I?'

And then Ian's head came up, and he looked around sharply. I didn't hear or see anything, but Linda and Ian were both staring up and down the street as though the bogeyman was coming to get them. I moved away from the wall and looked around me, and that was when I realized the street was empty. I was sure there had been people around when we went into the library, but now there wasn't a soul to be seen anywhere. And no traffic on the road, either. A hush had descended; just like the night before.

'Where did everybody go?' said Penny.

'What's happening?' said Linda.

'There's something in the street with us,' Ian said quietly. 'I can't see it, but it's here.'

I strained my hearing against the quiet, but couldn't hear anything apart from the heartbeats of the three people around me. There wasn't even a feeling of being watched. But Linda and Ian were actually shaking. They looked like they wanted to run but couldn't work out which direction would be safe. Linda's face was pale and strained. Ian's was covered in sweat.

Penny and I moved to stand back to back, a standard defensive position we'd practiced so often it was practically instinctual.

'Can you see anything?' Penny said quietly. 'Hear anything?'

'No,' I said.

'Glad it's not just me. Could it be the invisible demon at last?'

'I'm not picking up anything.'

'But you were certain you'd know it was there,' said Penny.

'I'm not certain anything is here,' I said.

'They are.'

Ian pushed Linda back against the library wall, and placed himself in front of her, protecting her with his body. Linda let him do it. Their eyes darted this way and that, like children who'd wandered into a bad place and found the monster was real after all. I couldn't do anything to protect them, because I couldn't see anything to protect them from. We all stood very still, bracing ourselves for an attack . . . until the moments dragged by, and nothing happened, and slowly we all began to relax. Everyone's heartbeat returned to normal, their breathing slowed, and the scent of fear disappeared from the air. Whatever might or might not have been threatening us had passed on by. Linda laughed raggedly, and then leaned forward and kissed Ian on the top of his head.

'I can always depend on you.'

'Of course you can,' said Ian. 'That's what I'm here for.'

'I don't love you, Ian. And I never will.'

'I know that.'

Linda pushed him forward, and stepped away from the wall. 'I think being stuck in a crazy town is driving us crazy too.'

'What did you think was here?' said Penny.

'I don't know,' said Ian. 'It felt like drowning . . .'

'Let's get out of here,' Linda said briskly. 'We're just spooking ourselves; and we still have work to do.'

'With you all the way,' said Ian.

They hurried off down the street. It was still empty. Maybe it was just that time of the day. I could see people hurrying by at the end of the street. Penny turned to look at me.

'OK, what the hell just happened?'

'Damned if I know,' I said. 'Either the town's mass hysteria is getting to us, or something else did.'

And that was when my mobile phone rang. We both jumped, just a little. I took the phone out of my pocket and stared at it.

'Aren't you going to answer that?' said Penny, after a while.

'Only the Colonel is supposed to know this number,' I said. 'And he was very clear we couldn't expect any support from the Organization.'

'You don't have to take the call,' said Penny.

'Yes I do,' I said. 'If only to find out who's ringing me.' I put the phone to my ear.

'Who is this?'

'It's Robert.'

'How did you get this number?'

'How do you think?' said Robert. 'Now shut up and listen. You have to come back to the church hall. Right now. There's been another murder.'

He rang off before I could ask who. I put the phone away and looked at Penny.

'I heard,' she said. 'Who do you think it is? There was no one in the hall, when we left.'

'Someone must have been lured back,' I said. 'Whoever it is, at least we know where we are now.'

'We do?' said Penny.

'One murder might be happenstance,' I said. 'But two is enemy action. Now we just have to figure out who the enemy is.'

We hurried back to the church hall. Striding it out without actually running, because that would have attracted attention. When we finally entered the hall Robert was standing with Inspector Godwin, looking at the bridesmaid Karen. She was standing over the wedding cake on its trolley. Her face had been forced down into the soft topping and held there until she suffocated. Her legs had locked in place, while her arms hung limply down. The sheer size of the cake was enough to hold her up as she leaned on it. Her pink fluffy outfit made her look like a doll that had been played with too

163

roughly, and then left for someone else to clear up.

Godwin glared at me. 'What are you doing here?'

'I called him,' said Robert. 'After I called you.'

'You're not needed,' said Godwin, including Penny in his glare. 'This is an official police investigation, and you're contaminating a crime scene just by being here.'

'I want him here,' said Robert. 'He can do things you can't.'

'You are working on your own, Inspector,' I said, carefully polite. 'You need all the help you can get. Two connected killings means there could be more to come.'

Godwin scowled at that, but didn't argue. I walked forward and studied the body thoughtfully, taking my time. Penny stuck close beside me. Karen's face had been pushed so deep into the soft icing, it had completely disappeared. But I still knew it was her. I recognized her scent.

'She hasn't been dead long,' I said. 'Maybe half an hour.'

'How can you be sure?' Godwin said immediately.

'Because it's been barely an hour since we were all here together,' I said.

'The cake was in the side room when we left,' said Robert. 'I found it out here, with Karen, when I came back to oversee setting up trestle tables for the wedding reception.'

'And you didn't see anyone?' said Godwin.

'No,' said Robert. 'I looked in the side room.

164

It was empty, the killer long gone. He'd made his point.'

'What point?' said Godwin.

'That no one connected to this wedding is safe,' said Penny. 'Someone really doesn't want it to happen.'

'But what was Karen doing back here?' I said. 'She was supposed to be at The Swan, helping Gillian and Tom with the guests.'

'How am I going to tell Gillian her best friend is dead?' said Robert.

'Would you like me to do it?' I said.

'No. It's a father's job.' Robert put out a hand to Karen's shoulder, as though to comfort her, and then drew it back again. 'I have called Gillian. She and Tom are on their way. I just told them someone else had been murdered. Didn't say who. It's not the kind of thing you should say over the phone.'

'You seem to be taking all of this very calmly, for a retired civil servant,' said Godwin.

'Shut up, Peter,' said Robert. He looked thoughtfully at the body. 'At least we can be sure now that the killings are connected to the curse.'

'And yet, neither of them look like the work of an invisible demon,' I said.

'The curse is cruel,' said Robert.

I didn't have an answer to that, so I concentrated on the body. 'An attack like this had to have taken strength, and determination. Karen would have struggled.'

'Unless the killer was invisible, and sneaked up on her,' said Penny. She looked quickly round

165

the room, as though to assure herself no one invisible was there with us.

'Why kill Karen?' I said. 'Of all the people involved with the wedding.'

'She was the most frightened,' said Robert. 'Maybe that attracted the killer.'

'And why do it here?' I said.

'The first body was found in the church,' said Penny. 'Now it's the church hall. It all comes back to the wedding. The killer is making a statement.'

'Like what?' said Godwin.

Penny shrugged. 'Getting married can be dangerous to your health? Or that of someone close to you.'

'But the killer still hasn't gone after the bride or groom,' I said. 'Which would be the quickest way to stop the wedding. And the curse has always been all about the bride and groom.'

'What do you think that means?' said Robert.

We all stopped and looked round, as Gillian and Tom burst in. Gillian saw Karen's body and let out a sick moan. Her knees started to buckle. Tom grabbed her, to hold her up. He didn't look away from the body. Gillian clung tightly to Tom as they came slowly forward.

'Get her out of that!' Gillian said suddenly. 'You can't just leave her like that! Get her out!'

'We really need to leave her there, for the time being,' Godwin said quickly. 'Let the crime scene specialists do their job. Every bit of trace evidence they can find is ammunition we can use to catch whoever did this.'

'Are you expecting anyone soon?' I said.

'I've put in a call,' said Godwin. 'Tagged it as urgent. Someone will be here as soon as they can.'

'This is all my fault,' said Gillian. 'I got Karen killed, by insisting on going ahead with the wedding. If I'd called it off she'd still be alive.'

'You can't know that,' said Tom.

'She was so frightened,' said Gillian. 'And I promised her she had nothing to be worried about.'

Tom tried to turn her away, so she wouldn't have to look at the body of her best friend, but she fought him till he stopped.

'She hated that cake,' said Gillian. 'She never said; but I could tell.'

'I need to ask you a few questions,' said Godwin.

'Not now!' said Tom. 'She's in shock. It can wait.'

Godwin started to argue, took in the look on Tom's face, and nodded reluctantly.

'It can wait.'

'We were both at The Swan,' said Tom. 'Surrounded by people. You can check.'

'I thought Karen was there with you?' I said.

'There wasn't anything useful for her to do,' said Gillian. 'So she went up to her room. To lie down for a while.'

'Then how did she end up here?' said Penny.

'I don't know,' said Gillian. 'She didn't have any reason to come back.'

'Someone must have told her she was needed here,' I said. 'Someone she trusted.'

167

Tom looked at me sharply. 'You think she knew her murderer?'

'That's usually the way,' I said.

'Dead because of me,' said Gillian. 'That's it. I'm calling off the wedding. I can't go through with it. Not after this.'

'No,' Tom said firmly. 'If we give in, whoever did this wins.'

'You think I care about that?' Gillian said fiercely. 'What if they kill someone else? What if they kill you?'

'We'll be perfectly safe as long as we stick together,' said Tom, keeping his voice carefully calm and reasonable. 'Once the marriage has taken place the killer won't have any reason to strike again. If we postpone the wedding for another day, what's to stop him coming after us again? Unless; you don't want to marry me.'

'I do,' said Gillian. 'You know I do.'

She stood a little straighter as her strength came back to her.

'All right; we go ahead,' she said. 'Because it's the only way to spit in the killer's face.'

'Holding the wedding could be like waving a red rag at a bull,' said Godwin. 'It could infuriate the killer into coming after you directly.'

'You'll be there to protect us,' said Gillian. 'And Ishmael and Penny. If someone comes lunging at us with a butcher's knife, I expect you to stop them.'

I left them arguing, and went prowling round the church hall. Checking out the scene with my more than human senses. I couldn't see or smell anything out of the ordinary. There were no footprints, no blood spots from a struggle, nothing left behind or obviously missing. I went back to look at the body. A thought occurred to me.

'I need to lift the face out of the cake,' I said. 'Just for a moment. I want to check whether her neck might have been broken, like the vicar.'

'You have no authority to interfere in this case!' Godwin said immediately. 'I won't have you compromising any evidence. As far as I'm concerned, you're just another suspect. So, as of now, I am ordering you to stay away from the wedding, and the Bergin family.'

'That's not going to happen,' I said.

'Then you're under arrest,' said Godwin. A pair of handcuffs suddenly appeared in his hand, as though he'd just been waiting for the opportunity.

'You can't arrest him!' said Penny. 'What's the charge?'

'Interfering with a police investigation,' said Godwin. 'Acting suspiciously, and not doing what he's told.'

Gillian and Tom objected, and Robert got into it too, but Godwin ignored them. His gaze was fixed on me, and his whole body was tense. He obviously wanted me to try something, so he could stop me. He was in good shape, but he didn't know what I could do. Penny was looking at me, expecting me to do something . . . But I would have had to call on my more than human strength and I couldn't risk that. It might have been what the beast within me was waiting for; an opportunity to break free, and break loose.

Godwin might get on my nerves, but I didn't want him dead. Or anyone else.

So I put forward my wrists, and Godwin snapped the cuffs on them. I knew he would have preferred to turn me around and cuff me from behind, but he was sensible enough to take the opportunity when it was offered. Penny looked at me with something like shock.

'Go ahead with the wedding,' I said to Gillian and Tom. 'Penny; stick with them. And don't worry about me.'

'Where are you taking him?' Penny said to Godwin, and her voice was cold enough to convince him to answer her.

'There's a holding cell in the local police station,' he said. 'He can cool his heels there, while I look into his background and find out who he really is.'

Penny started to say something about going with me, but I shook my head sharply, and she stopped.

'I'll get you bail, Ishmael,' said Robert, glaring at Godwin.

'Good luck finding anyone,' said Godwin. 'The town's gone into hiding, remember?'

He grabbed me by the arm and hustled me toward the door.

Eight
Invisible Demon

The sun was shining fiercely, not leaving a single shadow for me to hide in, as Inspector Godwin marched me through the narrow streets of Bradenford. Hauling me along by one arm so the handcuffs on my wrists were clearly visible to one and all. He kept a careful eye on me, to make sure I couldn't escape, while also being just a bit disappointed that I didn't even try. He would have taken any attempt to escape as an admission of guilt on my part, and justification for the way he'd treated me. He didn't know, couldn't know, that I didn't dare try anything for fear the beast inside me might break loose.

We passed through streets packed with people, nearly all of whom stopped to stare openly at me. They thought Godwin had captured the killer. Some looked relieved, some were angry it had taken so long; and some looked disappointed that I wasn't an invisible demon after all. But the general reaction still struck me as somehow . . . odd. No one shouted insults, or threats, and no one even tried to take a photo on their phone. They just stood where they were, staring silently, as Godwin and I passed by.

At least he was hurrying us along, probably because he wanted to get me locked away as soon as possible, and resisting the urge to show off the dangerous man he'd arrested single-handed. Of such things are careers made. I kept my face calm and impassive, but inside I was fighting not to fall apart. Being paraded in public, so everyone could get a good look at me, was my worst nightmare come true at last. I'd spent most of my life hiding in the shadows, ready to disappear completely at a moment's notice, shedding names and identities and even whole lives when necessary, just to make sure something like this could never happen. I took some comfort from the thought that Bradenford didn't have any surveillance cameras. At least there wouldn't be any record of this. And we were moving so quickly that most of the people who saw me would have a hard time describing me afterwards.

This was why I normally had enough sense not to take on cases in public places. There's a lot to be said for solving murders in isolated country mansions. The Organization knew that, which is why they saw to it that I always got assigned to such cases. I couldn't afford to be identified, or pinned down, to have the official authorities take an interest in my background. Because that would only lead to questions I couldn't answer, and perhaps a trip to Hazard Asylum. Or any of the other secret places that no one comes back from. I wondered if Robert would be the one to take me; for old times' sake. It was his fault I was here. His fault this was happening. But even so, I wouldn't wish some-thing like that on him.

172

As the inspector and I made our way down yet another street full of people, I raised my voice politely.

'Don't you have a car?'

'No,' said Godwin. 'Keep walking.'

'You could always call a taxi,' I said. 'I'm pretty sure they'd let you put it on expenses.'

'Stop talking,' said Godwin. 'We're almost there.'

'Of course we are,' I said. 'Nothing's ever far, in this town.'

The local police station turned out to be a characterless modern building, with no frills to take the edge off, tucked away down a side alley in someone's back yard. As though the town was ashamed of it, because it didn't fit in with their oldeworldey tourist-friendly facade. They didn't want to know what went on here. Godwin brought me to a halt before the front door, which bore a hastily handwritten note explaining that the station was closed temporarily. Godwin gave the door handle a good rattle, but it was locked. He glared at me like it was my fault.

'Stand there. Don't move.'

'Wouldn't dream of it,' I said.

He had to let go of my arm so he could search his pockets for the keys. I waited patiently, refraining from offering any helpful advice or comments. Godwin kept shooting glances at me as he moved from pocket to pocket, before finally producing a key ring with half a dozen keys on it. He looked at me suspiciously, clearly wondering why I was taking all of this so calmly.

He studied the keys dubiously, chose one and tried it in the lock, and couldn't hold back a sigh of relief when the lock turned. He pushed the door open and pushed me inside, crowding quickly in behind me. He then closed and locked the door. The sound of the lock turning was terribly cold and final. Like the end of a life.

The reception area was small and functional and completely deserted. All the lights were still on, suggesting the previous occupants had left in something of a hurry. Posters thumb-tacked to the wall behind the desk advertised all the usual anti-crime initiatives and support groups. Along with details of an upcoming fun run for charity; costumes optional. Everything was painted in the standard institutional colours; grey and green. It was hard to tell which looked more grim. I often wonder what effect that has on the poor souls who have to work there every day. A thought struck me and I turned to Godwin, who was still frowning at the keys on his ring.

'Why did everyone have to go, to fight the chemical fire?' I said. 'I mean; why take the receptionists and the typists and . . . everyone?'

'When the boat is leaking that badly, it's every hand to the pumps,' said Godwin. 'At least until they can get the professionals in.'

He realized he was talking politely to me, scowled fiercely to re-set the balance, and hauled me down a narrow corridor to the single holding cell. There were helpful arrows on the wall to point the way. I was tempted to dig my heels in, just to show I couldn't be moved unless I chose to be, but I didn't. The door to the holding cell turned out to be locked as well, and Godwin had to go through his routine with the key ring again. He peered uncertainly at the lock, and then at the keys.

'I should try that one,' I said helpfully, after a while.

'Shut up,' said Godwin, and then tried the key I'd indicated.

The door opened, and Godwin pushed me through. It was just a small featureless room with no window, a very basic table and two chairs. Godwin gestured harshly at the nearest chair.

'Yes,' I said. 'It's a chair. I have used one before.'

'Shut up. But before you sit down, give me your phone and your wallet.'

'Don't have them,' I said easily. 'I passed them to Penny, just before we left.'

'I didn't see you do that!'

I smiled. 'That's sort of the point. I'm not cooperating in this charade, for very good reasons. Which are of course none of your business.'

'Hold still,' said Godwin. 'I'm going to search you. Do you have anything about your person that might be dangerous? Blades, needles, that sort of thing?'

'No,' I said. 'But you'd better be careful anyway.'

'Why?'

'I'm ticklish.'

He looked like he really wanted to say something, but wouldn't lower himself. He had me raise my arms, and then frisked me quickly and thoroughly. He didn't find anything. All my pockets were empty. First rule of the spy game; never carry anything the enemy can use against you. Godwin stepped back, gestured for me to lower my arms, and looked at me blankly.

'What kind of man doesn't even have a handkerchief?'

'One who never catches colds,' I said. Which was perfectly true.

'Stay here,' he said. 'I'm going to make some phone calls about you.'

'Aren't you going to take the handcuffs off?'

'No.'

He backed out of the room, not taking his eyes off me, and then slammed the door and locked it. I sat down at the table, facing the door. I was so tired I could hardly keep my eyes open. As long as I had something to do, someone to fight, I could stay focused; but now it was just me and the empty room. I looked around. It didn't take long. I'd spent my life using all kinds of tricks and strategies to avoid ending up in a room like this, and it had all been for nothing. Beaten in the end not by any enemy, but by my own insufficiently buried past.

The room looked just like I'd always thought it would. Like a cage for a captured beast, or a box for an interesting new specimen. Somewhere secure to hold me, until the experts arrived. I was surprised I wasn't as scared as I'd always thought I'd be, when the hammer finally fell. In fact, I felt strangely calm. As though this was the inevitable end to the road I'd been travelling.

176

Perhaps I hadn't been running from this room all my life, but toward it. There was a certain sense of relief to the thought that the long chase was over; that I could finally stop running and rest. It might actually feel good, to look my captors in the face and say, *Here I am. You don't know what I am and neither do I. What are you going to do about it?* To be able to finally put down the mystery and burden of my life.

Except I couldn't do that; not while there were still people out there depending on me to save them from a killer.

I flexed my wrists in just the right way and the handcuffs sprang open. You can't work the spy game for as long as I have and not pick up a few useful tricks along the way. I arranged the handcuffs neatly on the tabletop, and looked at the door. I didn't need to get up to examine the lock; it was just a standard make. Getting out of the room would be easy, but after that . . . The station was too small for me to sneak out. No matter how quietly I moved. All Godwin had to do was be in the wrong place at the wrong moment and he'd be bound to see me. And then he'd try to stop me.

If we fought, and the beast got out . . . If I hurt him, or killed him . . . I couldn't let that happen. Godwin might annoy the hell out of me, but in the end he was just a man doing his job.

If I was going to get out of here, I had to find a way to bring Godwin onto my side. Which wasn't going to be easy, after the way I'd treated him. And thinking it was his own fault for being such a dick didn't help. But though I thought

177

and thought, and concentrated till my forehead ached, no viable plan presented itself.

There was nothing I could do that wouldn't make things worse. So I just sat there, and waited for Godwin to come back.

Time passed. I didn't look at my watch; that would just have made it worse. I could feel the presence of my alien self growing stronger, as I grew weaker. As though there was someone else in the room with me. My very own invisible demon, waiting patiently. Like a voice I couldn't quite hear, reminding me of how easy it would be to stop fighting and let it break me out. It could take care of Godwin, so I wouldn't have to. Godwin was a danger to both of us. He was going to want to take my photo, my fingerprints, maybe even a DNA sample. All the things I couldn't allow.

Godwin would be the death of me.

But I refused to be tempted. *Go back to sleep, old demon. I'm never going to let you out.* I was so tired . . . The need to sleep pressed down on me like a weight, and it was so much harder to fight back when there was nothing to do. I wanted to get to my feet and pace back and forth, like any other animal in a cage, but I couldn't allow any cracks in my self-control. Nothing my other self might take advantage of.

Finally, I heard Godwin coming back down the corridor. He unlocked the door and stood there for a moment, looking at me. Finally, he sat down on the opposite side of the table. His face gave nothing away, but at least he didn't have a file in his hands; which suggested his initial enquiries hadn't turned up anything useful about me.

'Don't I get a cup of tea?' I said.

'No. Do I look like your social worker?'

I looked at him carefully. 'Not really, no.'

Godwin finally noticed the empty handcuffs lying on the table. He looked at them blankly, and then at me. He started to say, 'How . . .?' and then stopped himself with an effort, refusing to be sidetracked.

'It doesn't matter. You're not going anywhere. Now, who are you, really? And I want your real name, not that Ishmael Jones nonsense.'

'This conversation isn't going to go anywhere you want,' I said.

'I'll be the judge of that.'

'While we're wasting time with this, the real killer is still out there,' I said sharply. 'And the Bergin family is still in danger.'

'I have nothing to lead me to the killer, nothing out of the usual in this town, except you,' said Godwin. 'You know something. I can tell. And you're not going anywhere until you tell me.'

'There's nothing useful I can tell you.'

'You'll talk to me, or . . .'

I raised an eyebrow. 'Or what, Inspector Godwin?'

And there must have been something in my voice, that made Godwin look at me differently. Not a threat, just a complete confidence that I didn't feel in any way threatened by him. Godwin seemed to realize for the first time that he was alone in a room with someone who wasn't in handcuffs any longer, and might be just a little more dangerous than he looked. To his credit, Godwin didn't give an inch. He just sat there, meeting my gaze steadily.

'I can keep you here till the real interrogators get back,' he said. 'And sooner or later, we will identify you. Find out who you are and where you're from, and what you're doing here.'

'No you won't,' I said.

And again, something in my voice stopped him. He could hear the truth in my words, and it threw him.

'Are you about to tell me you've got connections?' he said harshly. 'Like Mr Bergin?'

'No,' I said. 'Not like him.'

And that was when Godwin's mobile phone rang. He snatched it out, angry at being interrupted, and turned it off without even looking at the caller ID. Before he could put it back in his pocket, the phone rang again. Godwin turned it off again, more carefully this time. But even as he looked at it, the phone turned itself back on and rang a third time. Godwin looked at me. I shrugged. Godwin looked at the caller ID, but it was blank.

'Well?' I said. 'Aren't you going to answer that?'

He scowled at me. 'Is this something to do with you?'

'I really don't see how,' I said.

He put the phone to his ear. 'Who is this?'

And I heard the Colonel's dry clipped tones on the other end of the phone.

'I'm the man in charge. Now let Ishmael Jones

go, Detective Inspector Godwin, there's a good chap. He's not your man. And please don't bother him again.'

'I have good reason to detain him,' Godwin said stubbornly. 'Why should I listen to you?'

'Albion Blue Seven,' said the Colonel.

All the colour drained out of Godwin's face. He almost dropped the phone. That particular security code was one no working copper ever wanted to hear. It meant: Hands off, back away, you do not want to be involved in this if you like having a career. Because the needs of National Security will always trump those of law enforcement.

'All right,' said Godwin. 'I know when I'm beaten.'

'I should hope so,' said the Colonel. 'Now please pass your phone over to Mr Jones.'

Godwin did so numbly. I took the phone.

'How did you know I was in trouble, Colonel?'

'All part of the job.'

'I thought I was on my own here,' I said carefully.

'Officially, you are,' said the Colonel. 'But I owed you a favour and this is me paying it off. So please, solve your mystery and get the hell out of that dreary little backwater town. Because I won't be allowed to interfere again.'

The phone went dead. I handed it back to Godwin, and he put it away without even looking at it. He was staring at me as though he'd never seen me before; or at least wished he hadn't.

'Sorry about that,' I said.

'Who are you? Really?' said Godwin.

'Trust me,' I said. 'You don't want to know.'

I started to get to my feet, took in the look on Godwin's face, and sat down again. I'd been helped out of my predicament, but he hadn't. And I still thought I could use his help. He scowled at me sullenly.

'What do you want? You've won. Proved I can't touch you. You are free to go, Mr Jones; but if you're waiting for an apology you've got a long wait coming. I just did my duty.'

'Well, more or less,' I said. 'Look, we're on the same side, Inspector.'

'Doesn't feel that way from where I'm sitting.'

'I'm here to protect the Bergin family, and find out who the killer is,' I said. 'Just like you.'

'If you're about to suggest we work together, you can . . .'

'Not side by side,' I said. 'We'd end up killing each other before the murderer could get to us. But we could still attack the problem from different directions. I'll stick close to Gillian and Tom and keep them safe, while you use your official resources to dig into the backgrounds of everyone connected with the wedding. I can stay close, while you take the long view. I'm pretty sure I can keep Gillian and Tom alive until they're properly married.'

'They already are,' said Godwin.

'What?' I said.

He smiled, pleased he knew something I didn't. 'I already heard from Gillian. She and Tom decided it was too dangerous to wait till the afternoon, so they brought the ceremony forward. Gillian and Tom are now wife and husband, which means they're safe from the killer. And your protection isn't needed any longer.'

I sat there for a moment, considering what had changed and what hadn't.

'If this is all about the curse,' I said finally, 'then they won't be safe until they're past the wedding night. They still need guarding. But . . . if someone has just been using the curse as a smokescreen, to disguise their true intentions, then Gillian and Tom and everyone else connected to this marriage are still in danger. Either way, I'd better get back to them.' I looked at Godwin thoughtfully. 'Gillian said the two of you used to be close.'

'We were.'

'What happened?'

'What business is it of yours?'

I thought, but didn't say, *Because as an ex-boyfriend of hers, you could be a suspect. Did you pull strings, to be allowed to stay behind when everyone else left? Did you drag me away from Gillian to leave her defenceless?*

'Because it might be relevant,' I said. 'How can I know, until you tell me?'

And I sat and stared patiently at Godwin until he got the message that I wasn't going anywhere until I got an answer.

'We were both ambitious,' he said finally. 'But in different directions. One of us would have had to give up their plans to support the other; and it turned out both of us were too selfish to give up our dreams. So we went our separate ways. Probably for the best.'

'Do you still have feelings for her?' I said.

183

He smiled briefly, seeing where this was going. 'Not enough to kill people, to get her wedding called off. I just thought . . . this could be my last chance to do something for her. To impress her, and prove my ambitions had been worth pursuing. I called in every favour I was owed, to be allowed to stay behind. And perhaps . . . because despite all my years on the job, I've nothing to show for it. No big arrest, no career-making opportunities . . . If I could catch this murderer I could prove something to myself, as well as Gillian. Now go on, get the hell out of here. We both have things to do.'

I got to my feet. 'Don't worry. I'll look after Gillian and Tom.'

'They're married now. They're safe.'

'I don't think so,' I said.

I left him sitting there, staring at nothing. With his own invisible demon.

Nine
Green Monkeys

There's something about walking out of a police station that can't help but lift the spirits. When I'd been pushed through the door, with Godwin's hand on my arm and his cuffs on my wrists, I hadn't been sure I'd ever emerge from the station again as a free man. Though there was always the possibility I might have come back out with something else looking out from behind my eyes, and Godwin's blood dripping from my hands. One of us had just dodged a bullet, and I wasn't sure which of us had been luckiest. But I was out now, out and free, and for the moment at least my other self seemed to have retired to the back of my head. I couldn't feel its presence any more, and my thoughts were my own. Leaving me free to concentrate on the case I came here to solve.

I wasn't looking forward to walking back through the town. The last time the towns-people saw me it was as an arrested murderer. Once they saw me walking freely among them again, they might regard me as an escaped murderer. They might even raise the alarm, attack me, or run away screaming. All of which would be bound to attract even more attention I didn't want. The mood this town was in, there was no telling what they might do. And even if they did take me at face value, a man freed because he was innocent; I've never liked being stared at. I strode down the side alley, doing my best to appear ordinary and harmless, while bracing myself for a long walk in the public eye.

But when I emerged onto the main street, a very familiar-looking taxi was waiting for me. Cathy peered out of her side window and beamed at me cheerfully.

'Need a ride?'

I stopped and looked at her for a moment. 'How did you know to find me here?'

'Are you kidding?' said Cathy. 'News of your arrest is all the town's been talking about! They've been doing everything but putting up flags and bunting and dancing in the street. All right, I exaggerate. It's allowed; I'm a local character. But I knew it wouldn't be long before you found a way to get yourself released. You're no more a murderer than I am. So I just passed by this way on a regular basis, and waited for you to turn up. And here you are! Took a bit longer than I thought, but it's not like my services are much in demand at the moment.'

I wasn't sure I believed any of that. Godwin had me locked up in that holding cell for hours. And I was starting to find it just a bit suspicious how often I kept bumping into Cathy. Even in a town this small. I'd been looking for an invisible killer, and who would be harder to spot than a taxi driver? Someone who was always out and about, never needing to explain why they were anywhere . . . that had to make for the perfect disguise. Of course, Cathy was a bit loud to go entirely unnoticed, but that could be part of the cover. Perhaps she only showed people the face she wanted them to see, so they wouldn't guess what was hiding behind the mask.

And now, here she was again. If I got into the taxi, would anyone ever see me again? But then, why would Cathy want to kill me? Why would she want to kill anyone? Questions, questions, and never an answer in sight. I realized I'd been standing there for some time, just staring at Cathy while she waited patiently. I had to make up my mind, before she started asking questions I didn't want to answer. The taxi might be a trap or it might not, but it had to be better than walking back through the town, possibly pursued by an angry mob with flaring torches and assorted blunt instruments. I smiled easily at Cathy, and pulled open the front door.

'You don't mind if I ride up front?'

'Of course not,' said Cathy. 'Is it OK if I squeeze your thigh occasionally?'

'My girlfriend would rip your arm off and beat your head in with the wet end,' I said calmly.

'That would be a no, then,' said Cathy.

She slammed the taxi into gear and drove off, and we went plunging through streets that were surprisingly empty of traffic again.

I kept a careful eye on the town as we drove through it. There was hardly anyone about, and the few people hurrying along the pavements looked as though something was chasing them. The light was going out of the day as night crept up on it, and the town had that under siege feeling again. How long had I spent in that cell, waiting for Godwin to get to me? I finally allowed myself to look at my watch, and swore silently.

'Did you hear that Tom and Gillian are married?' said Cathy.

'The inspector told me,' I said. 'I suppose there must be a feeling of relief in the town now that's over?'

'Not really,' said Cathy. 'The happy couple still have to survive their wedding night. Let's just hope Tom isn't prone to first night nerves, and can perform under pressure.'

'What was the wedding like?' I said.

'Oh, it was wonderful!' said Cathy. 'If a bit rushed. Everyone involved was so worried something might interrupt the ceremony, they stripped it back to the bare bones. Went straight from "Here comes the bride" to "I do, I do" without even pausing for the "just cause and impediment" bit. Which was probably just as well; that dishy best man was so on edge I think he would have hammered anyone into the ground if they so much as coughed in the wrong place. But, it's all done now. Gillian got her big day, in front of a packed crowd of friends and family; and I got to be the bridesmaid after all! Since Karen couldn't do it.'

She glanced across at me. 'Given that you are running around unfettered and free, I'm assuming you were able to persuade the redoubtable Peter that you are entirely innocent?'

'It took a while,' I said. 'But he finally saw the light.'

'He's not usually that easy to persuade,' said Cathy.

'I was very convincing,' I said. 'Can I just ask, where are we going?'

'To The Swan,' said Cathy. 'It didn't seem right to hold the reception in the church hall; not after what happened there. I mean, yes, they had wheeled Karen and her cake into the side room, out of view, but everyone still knew she was there. Like the spectre at the feast. So Gillian and Tom decided to hold their little get together at The Swan. Though as it turned out they needn't have bothered. All the guests hit the road the moment the ceremony was over. You can't blame them. They didn't know what they were getting into till they got here. Hell, most of the town wouldn't be here if they had any choice in the matter.

'So, the friends and family said all the right things, kissed the bride and groom as quickly as they could get away with, and then got the hell out of Dodge before anything nasty could happen to them. And of course I won't be attending the reception. My boss wouldn't allow me to take the time off. He wouldn't have let me take time off to be bridesmaid, so I didn't tell him. The other drivers covered for me. No doubt the boss will find out eventually and shout at me a lot; but I'm used to that. He's my dad.'

We pulled up outside The Swan. I emerged from the taxi and looked up and down the empty street, while Cathy checked her meter and told me the fare. I added a generous tip, and Cathy looked at me.

189

'Not that I'm complaining, you understand, but what is that for?'

'If you're not on a call, don't go far,' I said. 'Hang around. I might have a use for you.'

'I'll bet you say that to all the taxi drivers,' said Cathy.

She dropped me a wink, laughed raucously, and sent the taxi roaring off into the gathering night. I didn't have any real reason to suspect her of anything, except having too much character for her own good, but I've always believed in keeping my suspects close, where I can keep an eye on them. I strode into The Swan, wondering exactly who would be there to greet me.

Nettie was still sitting behind her reception desk, leafing through *Vogue* and scratching under her wig with the blunt end of a biro. She put on her professional smile as she heard someone come in, and then made a shocked sound when she saw who it was. She jumped to her feet, and then didn't seem to know whether she should stand her ground and welcome me back or drop down and hide under the desk until I was gone. I gave her my best reassuring smile.

'So!' she said. 'You're here . . . I thought, I mean we all thought . . .'

'It was just a silly misunderstanding,' I said smoothly. 'The inspector and I talked it through, and now we're the best of chums.'

'Well, that's nice, dear,' Nettie said hesitantly.

'Where's the wedding reception?' I said.

'In the bar, dear,' said Nettie. 'I did offer them the use of my function room, but since there were so few people the bar seemed more appropriate. Tom very kindly said he'd cover the cost of all the food I ordered, so that's in the bar too. Though most of it will probably go to waste. Such a shame . . . You go on through to the bar, dear. Eat as much as you can. Someone should. And help yourself to a drink. I'm afraid my Albert is off with his friends, somewhere, but I'll send him through to help out as soon as I see him.'

'Something to look forward to,' I said.

I went into the bar. A Carpenters compilation was playing over the speakers, and the tables had been pushed back to allow Gillian and Tom to slow dance in the middle of the room. Penny, Robert and David were leaning on the bar with drinks in front of them, looking dubiously at the mountains of finger food piled up on the bar top. They'd all changed out of their wedding outfits and back into everyday clothes. Penny looked round and saw me standing in the doorway. She grinned broadly, yelled my name and ran to me.

She hit me so hard she would have knocked me off my feet if I hadn't braced myself, and then hugged me tightly like she'd never let me go. I held on to her like a drowning man going down for the third time. Over her shoulder I could see Gillian and Tom had stopped dancing to stare at us. They looked like they didn't know what to say. David looked surprised; Robert didn't. Penny and I finally broke apart. She punched me hard in the arm, and glared at me.

'What took you so long? It's been hours! I was starting to get worried!'

191

'The situation was complicated,' I said. 'But it's all been sorted now. The inspector won't bother us again.'

'Good,' said Penny. 'I'd already decided if you didn't show up soon, I was going to break you out myself. I was ready to knee that man so hard in the groin he'd be able to use his balls for earmuffs.'

'Good thinking, spy girl.'

'You're welcome, space boy.'

'I hate cutesy nicknames,' said David.

I put my arm around Penny and we went forward to join the others. Gillian and Tom looked at me as though they'd never expected to see me again. David appeared completely thrown, and Robert was just smiling quietly, as though my triumphant return was nothing more than what he'd expected. Penny handed me my phone and wallet, and I tucked them away about my person again.

'Fast thinking,' she said quietly.

'Years of experience,' I said.

'Is everything really all right now?' said Penny. 'What's happening with the inspector?'

'He didn't have anything he could use to hold me,' I said. 'He just felt the need to be seen to be doing something.'

'Typical Peter,' said Gillian. 'Even at school he always had to put on a show, to make it look like he knew what he was doing. Even when we were dating.'

'I won't ask,' said Tom.

'Best not to,' said Gillian.

'I'm sorry I missed the wedding,' I said. 'Congratulations. Did everything go as planned?'

'Oh, it was marvellous!' said Penny. 'The church was full of candles, and flowers, and not a mad killer or invisible demon to be seen anywhere.'

'Best kind of wedding,' I said.

'But the killer is still out there, somewhere,' Robert said flatly.

That thought stopped everyone, for a moment. They all looked at each other, until David got to the point.

'So . . . we're still in danger?'

'We got through the wedding,' said Robert. 'That's what matters.'

Tom forced a smile for me. 'Come and kiss the bride, Ishmael. You might as well. Everyone else has. Even if they couldn't find the guts to stick around for the reception.'

I kissed Gillian on the cheek, and smiled at her. 'Was your big day everything you wanted it to be?'

'Yes,' she said. 'Some of the details had to be abandoned, under duress, but everything went as it should. Even if all my specially-invited friends and family took off, first chance they got.'

'They were here to see you married,' said Robert. 'Settle for that. And don't bother sending them thank-you notes for the presents.'

'More food for the rest of us!' Tom said valiantly.

'Help yourself,' said David. 'I couldn't manage

another pineapple chunk if you put a gun to my head.'

'I don't see the Reverend Stewart,' I said.

Robert sniffed loudly. 'Not him. He pissed off back to his own parish the moment the ceremony was over. Apparently doing his duty only went so far.'

'I think he was a bit put out at how fast we rushed through the wedding,' said Tom. 'And he probably didn't like the way Gillian and I glared at him, every time he tried to slow it down.'

'We told him, no hymns,' growled Gillian.

And then the two of them smiled at each other, moved back to the middle of the room, and resumed slow dancing. Staring into each other's eyes. Penny and I joined Robert and David at the bar. Penny was holding onto my arm with both hands, as though to make sure we couldn't be separated again. David poured me a glass of champagne.

'Not a vintage so much as a decent effort,' he said. 'But it's drinkable. Not much of a reception, is it? I never even got a chance to give my best man's speech.'

'Let us be grateful for small mercies,' said Robert.

David gave him a wounded look. 'I worked hard on that speech!'

'I already know all I need to about Deirdre Turner, thank you.'

'I was joking!'

'Some things you don't joke about,' said Robert.

'Is Gillian really happy, about how her wedding turned out?' I said.

'I think so,' said Robert. 'In the end it was the marriage that mattered, not the details. I could have told her that.'

'Even if she did make a fuss over the cake,' David muttered.

I looked at him. 'What?'

'She wanted to use her wedding cake!' said David. 'Even though her best friend had been smothered in it! It took a long time to talk her out of it. Though when I say talk, Robert ended up having to shout quite a bit.'

'I knew the cake was important to her, but it wouldn't have been right,' said Robert. 'Even if we did remove the top tier. Gillian did see that, eventually.'

David shuddered dramatically. 'I wouldn't have touched a slice, no matter what part of the murder weapon it came from.' And then he stopped, and smiled. 'Though if you thought that was a bit hard-hearted, it was nothing compared to what happened when Cathy turned up, wanting to be the replacement bridesmaid. Apparently she and Gillian were friends at school . . .'

'It was a very generous gesture,' Robert said firmly. 'And Gillian was very grateful. I'm sure it helped steady her, to have an old female friend there to lean on.'

'But Cathy wanted to take the pink dress off Karen's body, so she could wear it!' said David. 'Just so she wouldn't look out of place, as the only one not dressed up. That is all kinds of inappropriate.' He smiled again. 'Not that she could have squeezed into that frock, even if you used two tire levers and a jar of Vaseline. Karen was a big girl, but Cathy looks like she could wrestle professionally. Against men. And win. In the end, Gillian just had to say no. Loudly.'

'Cathy always was a bit . . . extreme,' said Robert.

'Really?' I said. 'In what way?'

'Man mad,' said Robert. 'From the time she was old enough to know the difference, and know it meant something. I was worried some of that might rub off on Gillian, when they started hanging out together at school; but Gillian always had a hard head on her shoulders. Whereas Cathy only ever wanted to be . . .'

'Popular?' I said.

'Aye,' said Robert. 'That's one way of putting it.'

I thought about that. David finished his champagne, and immediately poured himself another glass.

'It was a shame, what happened to Karen,' he said. 'Her death really got to me. I mean, I hardly knew her; but I did know her. Which was more than I could say for the Reverend Allen.'

I picked up something in his voice when he spoke about the vicar, so I raised an eyebrow. David saw that Robert was looking a bit uncomfortable, and smiled coldly.

'I'm sorry the man is dead, of course I am, but we never took to each other. Everyone always thought he was so nice, but he didn't waste any time making it clear he disapproved of people like me. People of my persuasion. He couldn't even bring himself to use the word gay. Though

196

I think he might have used the word deviant, if he thought he could get away with it.'

He took a good drink from his glass, while Robert looked somewhere else.

'I think I'm supposed to change the subject,' said David. He looked at me thoughtfully. 'Two people dead, and the murderer is still out there somewhere. Do you think Tom and Gillian are safe, now they're married?'

'Not till we get them through the wedding night,' I said. 'Once that's past, the curse won't be any kind of threat. With that out of the way, we should be able to see the killer more clearly.'

'You still think it's a human killer?' said Robert.

'Don't you?' I said.

Robert looked into his glass, but didn't drink from it.

'I don't know what I believe any more,' he said. 'All I know for certain is that my daughter is in danger. And my new son-in-law, of course. Until I'm sure about what's really going on, I can't properly defend either of them. I could handle a human killer . . .'

'You could?' said David.

Robert glared at him. 'I'm not dead yet. I know a thing or two. And I could take you with both legs strapped behind my back. I will fight to defend my daughter, or die to protect her, if need be.'

'Except hopefully you won't have to,' I said. 'That's why I'm here.'

'But what about after tonight?' Penny said carefully. 'We can't bodyguard Tom and Gillian forever, waiting for the killer to strike.'

'I don't think the killer will let things get that far,' I said. 'One way or another, I'm pretty sure he'll strike again before the night is over.'

'Why?' said Penny.

'Because he's driven,' I said. 'He wanted to stop Tom and Gillian getting married, and now that's failed, all that's left to him is to make sure the marriage can't continue. The only way to be sure of that is to kill one or both of them. And he has to do it on the wedding night, so their deaths can still be blamed on the curse.'

'So what do we do?' said Robert, practical as always.

'I don't want Gillian and Tom staying at The Swan tonight,' I said flatly. 'This place is far too difficult to defend. Too many ways in and out, and too many corridors. There's no way we could cover all of them. Even if we set up guard outside their room, a hotel this old is bound to have any number of hidden doors and secret passageways. The only way to be sure of keeping them safe would be to stay in the room with them. Which probably would not go down well, on their wedding night. We need to take them back to your house, Robert. It's isolated, so we can see and hear anyone coming. There's only a front and a back door to keep an eye on, and a lot less space to cover. Is that all right with you?'

'Of course it is,' Robert said gruffly. 'But you'll have to talk Gillian into it. She has reasons for not wanting to stay at the house. Feel free to throw a real scare into both of them, if that's what it takes.'

'I can do that,' I said.

I went over to Gillian and Tom, who reluctantly stopped dancing. I explained my plan, and the reasons behind it, and they surprised me by agreeing immediately.

'I've never felt safe in that hotel room,' said Tom.

'We'd definitely be better off at Dad's place,' said Gillian.

'It seems such a long time since I felt safe,' said Tom. 'For me, or for you. And I was so happy when you agreed to marry me.'

'I should never have come back here,' said Gillian. 'Just to fulfil a dream I had as a teenager. To prove to the town I was someone, after all.'

'You couldn't have known any of this would happen,' said Tom.

'I knew about the curse,' said Gillian.

Tom stared at her. 'You always said you didn't believe in it.'

'I don't,' said Gillian. 'But I think it believes in us.'

Tom turned to look at me. 'Just give us time to pack our bags, and we can be ready to leave any time.'

'There's no need to rush,' I said. 'I don't think anything will happen while it's still daylight. Too easy for our killer to be seen. And this bar is far too public a place to allow anyone to sneak up on you, like he did the others. You're safe enough here for the time being; as long as none of you go wandering off on your own.'

Gillian put her arms around Tom. 'I am not letting you out of my sight until this nightmare is over.'

'We should stay here as long as possible,' I said. 'Let the killer think you're spending the night in the hotel. If we leave it to the last moment to relocate to Robert's place, that should throw the killer off balance and ruin his plans.'

'I'm all for that,' said Tom.

The reception continued, in a quiet kind of way. The Carpenters compilation ran out, and no one volunteered to start it up again or go look for something else. We addressed ourselves to the mountains of finger food, in a dutiful sort of way. It wasn't bad, but no one had much of an appetite. We were all thinking too much, about what might happen next. There was a lot of drinking.

I made a point of keeping up with everyone, so as not to stand out. But the alcohol didn't seem to be affecting anyone much. They were all drinking steadily, pacing themselves; because no one wanted to get drunk. For fear of finding themselves incapable of fighting back if the killer turned up. They were just drinking to take the edge off. David disappeared to the toilet several times. Tom just grinned when I pointed out that going off on your own wasn't a good idea.

'He always did have a bladder the size of a pea. I still remember the time he had to make a sudden exit while we were on stage one night, just before his character was about to announce who the murderer was. That called for some fast ad-libbing from the rest of us.' He shrugged unhappily. 'Fictional detectives always make it look so easy. Do you have any idea what's going on, Ishmael?'

'Not as such,' I said.

Robert took me off to one side, so we could speak quietly together.

'I did put in a call to Black Heir, right after you were arrested, to get them to intervene on your behalf. But they still hadn't got back to me when you came strolling through the door with a big grin on your face.'

'That was good of you,' I said. 'But did you really think Black Heir would get involved, to help me out?'

'They'd have done it for me, after all the things I did for them,' said Robert. 'Or I'd have known the reason why. How did you cope with Peter? He doesn't normally let go once he's got his teeth into something.'

'The Organization phoned Godwin,' I said. 'And put the hard word on him.'

'Of course they did,' said Robert. He looked at me thoughtfully. 'What are they like to work for? I never knew much about them, even when I was working in the field. I heard stories, of course, but . . .'

'The first rule about the Organization,' I said, 'is that you don't talk about the Organization.'

Robert nodded. 'That's what I heard. So, what's Peter doing now? Any chance of him showing up here? He might not be the brightest button in the box, but we could use another pair of eyes. And fists. Peter always was a scrapper.'

'I asked him to check into the background of everyone involved with the wedding,' I said.

'Mostly to keep him busy, but there was always the chance his official resources would turn up something.'

David opened another bottle of champagne, and I allowed him to freshen my glass. He was getting through a fair amount of the stuff, but seemed to be pissing it away as fast as it went down. His eyes were still clear and his voice was still steady. He just seemed a little more sure of his opinions, along with a growing tendency to stab the air with a finger to back them up.

'Champagne doesn't do anything to me,' he said. 'It's like water, in the theatre. I'm just concerned that after Karen's death, I'm a target too. I only hope the marriage is worth it, after all this fuss.'

He didn't sound too convinced about that. I looked at him thoughtfully.

'How do you mean?'

'I tried to talk Tom out of going ahead with the wedding,' said David. 'Given that most of his relationships break up fast enough, once things start getting serious. Tom always was flighty.'

Tom appeared suddenly beside him. 'Keep your voice down! Do you want Gillian to hear?'

'Sorry,' David said immediately, peering at Tom just a bit owlishly. 'Didn't mean to upset her. Or you.'

'Gillian's been through enough today,' said Tom. 'And need I remind you; most of your relationships crashed and burned too.'

David shrugged. 'Still haven't found the right

202

man. Though I have looked in some very interesting places. Tom . . . you know I only want
you to be happy, right?'

'I know that,' said Tom.

'I just don't want you to be hurt again.'

'I won't be. I got it right this time.' Tom
clapped a hand on David's shoulder. 'You do
know we'll still be friends now I'm married?
I'm not going to cut you off, or disappear from
your life.'

'But it won't be the same,' said David. 'How
could it be? But . . . none of that matters.' He
looked steadily at Tom. 'When you go back to
Robert's place, I'm going with you. To make sure
nothing happens to you. If that's all right . . .'

'It'll be good to have you there,' said Tom.
'I'll feel a lot safer, having someone around I
know I can depend on.'

'That's me,' said David. 'Dependable. I'll look
out for you, Tom. Just like I always have.'

Tom smiled, clapped David on the shoulder
again, and went back to Gillian. David looked
after him.

'I'm not usually like that,' he said to me. 'So
petty. I think . . . I'm just jealous. That he could
have a day like this, and I never will. Gays can
get married these days, but not like Tom and
Gillian. No ritual that goes back centuries, no
public acclaim, no being just like everyone else.'

He emptied his glass, and poured himself more
champagne. 'Unlike Tom, I never had any great
ambitions to be an actor. I only went into the
theatre to meet other men like me. It was either
that or fashion; and I wasn't that bitchy. I just

203

wanted somewhere I could feel at home. No one was more surprised than me when I became something of a success. But outside of the business . . .'

He stopped abruptly, and looked at me. 'Do you know the story of the green monkey?'

'No,' I said. 'I don't think I do.'

'Scientists took a group of monkeys who'd been raised together, and kept in the same cage all their life. The scientists removed one monkey, took it out of sight and dyed its fur green. Then they put it back in the cage. And the other monkeys killed it. Tore it to pieces, screaming with rage and horror. Because it was different. And that's me.'

He stared broodingly into his glass. 'I could pass, you know. A lot of actors do. I could act so straight no one would ever guess. But I decided a long time ago that I would never give up being me, just to fit in.'

'I know what you mean,' I said.

He looked at me. 'You do?'

'I'm not gay,' I said. 'But I do have a lot of experience when it comes to not fitting in. Never feeling at home, always on the outside, looking in.'

'Why?' said David. 'What's so different about you?'

I look human, but I'm not. I'm a spy who doesn't officially exist, working for an Organization that doesn't exist. I'm a monster who fights monsters.

'I'm an illegal alien,' I said. 'Don't tell anyone.'

At which point, Nettie stuck her head through the open door and cleared her throat loudly.

'Sorry to interrupt, dears, but there's a phone call for Mr Jones.'

Penny and I looked at each other. There were all kinds of reasons why that wasn't necessarily a good thing. Robert was looking at me worriedly. I smiled at him reassuringly.

'It's probably just Inspector Godwin, with some information I asked him to find for me.'

Everyone went back to their drinking. I gestured for Penny to stay and keep an eye on everyone, and then followed Nettie back into reception. She handed me the reception phone as though bestowing a prize. I nodded my thanks, and then looked steadily at her until she moved away to dust something that didn't need dusting and give me the illusion of privacy.

'Inspector Godwin?' I said into the phone.

'No, this is Linda. You remember, the reporter.'

'What do you want, Linda? And how did you know I was here?'

'Oh please, you can't hide anything in this town. Look, I need you to come and meet me at Trinity Church. Right now. I've found out something.'

'Is it important?' I said, glancing back at the bar.

'It might explain a lot,' she said. 'I was trying to dig up some dirt on everyone connected to the wedding, as a way of getting back for being banned, but there didn't seem to be any. No one had a bad word to say about anyone. Very frustrating, for a working journalist. I was thinking about making up something juicy and selling it to the tabloids. The local people would know

205

it wasn't true, but the tabloids wouldn't care. But then I stumbled across something I didn't expect. Something I need to talk to you about. Can you come straight away?'

'Just to discuss some gossip about someone in the wedding party?' I said. 'Can't you come here? We have drinks.'

'Oh no,' Linda said immediately. 'Not there. It wouldn't be safe. You come here. And you're the only one I can trust with this, so come alone.'

'I don't go anywhere without Penny,' I said flatly.

'All right! Bring her! But hurry; I don't feel safe. Not with what I know.'

She rang off. I cradled the phone, and then tapped it thoughtfully. Wondering what on earth Linda could know that I didn't. Nettie stopped pretending to dust, and drifted a little closer.

'Was it important, dear?'

'Hard to tell,' I said. 'You can have your desk back now, Nettie.'

'Thank you, dear. It's not like I'm using it for much.'

I went back into the bar, and gestured for Penny to come and join me. She hurried over, and the others broke off their conversations to watch us. I quietly brought Penny up to speed, and she shook her head immediately.

'I don't like this, Ishmael. What if this big secret she's discovered is something about you?'

'Loath as I am to admit it, not everything is about me,' I said. 'She wants me to come to her because what she's found out scares her. And

206

given that I still don't have a single clue to point to the murderer . . .'

'All right,' said Penny. 'Let's go.' She smiled suddenly. 'She did seem very taken with you. Maybe this is her idea of an assignation. Don't worry, I'll protect you if she tries to jump you.'

'You're so good to me,' I said.

'Yes, I am,' said Penny. 'And don't you forget it.'

I turned to address the others. 'Penny and I are just nipping out for a few moments. None of you are to go anywhere until we get back, or go off on your own . . . Oh hell, where's David?'

'In the toilet again,' said Tom. 'Don't worry, I'll tell him what he missed when he gets back.'

'Are we in any danger?' said Robert.

'Not right now,' I said. 'But no one's safe until this is over.'

'OK, that's it,' said Tom. 'We are getting out of here. Gillian and I are relocating to Robert's place, the moment our bags are packed.'

'Leave your bags where they are,' I said sternly. 'We don't want anyone to know you're leaving. None of you are to stir from this bar till we come back. And if you get a message that seems to come from me, don't believe it. If I don't say it to you in person, you don't listen.'

'Are you always this paranoid?' said Gillian.

'The killer is getting close to his end game,' I said. 'And, he's getting more desperate. There's no telling what he might do.'

'Dear God, I want to hit someone,' said Tom.

'Me too,' said Gillian.

'Go,' Robert said to me. 'I'll hold the fort here.'

'Of course you will,' I said.

Penny and I hurried through reception, nodding quickly to Nettie as we passed. She flashed us her professional smile.

'Have a nice evening, dears.'

'That,' Penny said quietly as we left through the front door, 'has to be the triumph of optimism over experience.'

Once we were outside I looked up and down the street. The night sky was dark and starless, and the street lamps shed their amber glow like so many uncaring eyes. There was no one about, and no traffic on the road.

'What are you looking for?' said Penny. 'The invisible demon?'

'I asked Cathy to stick around in case we needed her,' I said. 'But there's no sign of her taxi anywhere.'

'She's probably got a fare,' said Penny. 'It's not like we're paying her a retainer. Come on, we can walk to the church. It's not far.'

And then we smiled at each other, because we knew we were both thinking the same thing: *It's not far, because nothing ever is in this town.*

We strode quickly through streets that were empty because everyone else thought it was too dangerous to be out; and I had to wonder if they might be right. Our footsteps rang out loudly on the quiet.

'You'd think the townspeople would feel safer, now the marriage has taken place,' said Penny.

'They believe in the curse,' I said. 'And that's always been more about what happens on the wedding night. They don't believe it's over yet.'

'But if they believe the curse is specifically targeting Gillian and Tom, why are they so afraid?'

'Because of what happened to the vicar, and Karen,' I said. 'They think the curse is spilling over onto other people.'

'Because . . .?'

'The curse is cruel,' I said.

I preferred the empty streets. If only because I really wasn't in the mood to be stared at. Penny knew what I was thinking. She slipped her arm through mine and hugged it against her side.

'Being dragged off in cuffs like that . . . it must have been awful for you.'

'It was,' I said. 'But I've been through worse.'

'I should have made Godwin take me with you,' said Penny. 'I was ready to go; till I saw you shake your head. Why didn't you want me with you? I hated thinking of you being locked up in some cell, all alone.'

And I thought, but didn't say: *I didn't want you with me because I was worried about what I might have to do, to break free. I didn't want you to see me like that.*

'I thought I might find it easier to convince Godwin to let me go, if there wasn't anyone there to see him back down,' I said.

'Are there likely to be any records of you being held in custody?' said Penny. 'Anything we need to worry about?'

'After the scare the Organization put into

Godwin, he'll know it's in his best interests to destroy any paperwork,' I said.

'Why did they do that for you?' said Penny. 'After they made such a big deal of saying we were on our own here?'

'They didn't,' I said. 'The Colonel did. Because he said he owed me.'

'Oh . . .' said Penny. 'That was nice of him.'

I wasn't so sure. In my experience, favours always come with a price tag.

We got to Trinity Church quickly enough. The street outside was deserted, but there were lights on inside the church.

'Probably candles left over from the wedding,' said Penny. 'I wish you could have seen it, Ishmael.'

'Me too,' I said.

We moved round the side of the church, to the front door. It was standing wide open. We stood and looked at it for a moment.

'You did break the lock,' said Penny. 'But even so . . .'

'Yes,' I said. 'Even so.'

I slipped inside, with Penny right behind me. Candles burning in every niche filled the church with a warm, honeyed glow. It would have been a cheerful sight, if it hadn't been for Linda. She was bent over the font, not moving. Her face had been forced down into the water and held there till she drowned. So the body would be the first thing anyone saw when they entered the church. Penny made a low, shocked sound. I looked quickly round the church, my eyes piercing the shadows, to make sure we were alone, and then I moved forward to examine the murder scene. There was water splashed around the base of the font, suggesting a struggle. Linda had fought for her life; right till the end.

'This is just like Karen, and the wedding cake,' said Penny, doing her best to sound calm and composed. 'Maybe the killer is a demon after all. The curse is cruel.'

'People can be cruel too,' I said.

'I wonder what she would have told us . . .'

'We got here too late,' I said. 'If Cathy had only been there with her taxi . . .'

'It wasn't her fault,' said Penny. 'And it wasn't ours, either. We had no way of knowing.'

'The killer is always one step ahead of us,' I said. 'As though he knows what we know.'

'Such an awful way to die,' said Penny. 'Ishmael, what does it say about us, that we've encountered so many bodies something like this barely affects us?'

'It says we're professionals,' I said. 'And all the more determined to catch the killer.'

I looked the body over carefully, without touching it.

'Linda said she knew something, and wanted to tell me what it was. She thought she was in danger, just for knowing it. The killer couldn't allow us to learn what she knew, so he got to Linda first and silenced her.'

'How did he get here before us?' said Penny. 'It was only a short walk.'

'More importantly, how did he know we were coming here?' I said. And then a thought struck

211

me, and I looked quickly around. 'Linda was a reporter; she might have written something down. See if you can spot a bag or a notebook anywhere.'

We searched all the pews, and behind the altar, but didn't find anything. I even had a quick look in the bell tower, and the single rope stared back at me accusingly, because I still didn't know who the murderer was. No bag, and no notebook. We went back to Linda's body.

'We should move her away from there,' said Penny. 'She looks so . . . undignified like that.'

'I'm pretty sure Inspector Godwin would say we were interfering with a crime scene.'

'Are we going to tell him about this?'

'I'll phone him when we get back to The Swan,' I said. 'Just before we leave for Robert's place. They're going to need us. Linda doesn't need anything, any more.'

'This happened after she spoke to you, but before we got here.' Penny said slowly. 'That's a limited envelope of opportunity. Maybe we passed the killer on the way here and didn't even know it.'

'I didn't see anyone,' I said. 'But maybe they went out of their way not to be seen, because they couldn't afford to be recognized.'

Penny looked at me sharply. 'You think the killer is someone we know?'

'That's usually how it works out, in cases like this,' I said. 'The more I look at how the murders were committed, the more I see personal involvement. Emotion, as well as necessity.'

'But why such extreme methods?' said Penny.

212

'I mean, he drowned Linda is just six inches of water! Why not simply break her neck, like he did with the vicar?'

'I think the first murder was planned,' I said. 'While the others were carried out in a hurry. This was done in anger, and with a need to horrify. He's putting on a show. *See what you made me do, because you wouldn't do what I wanted*! This was supposed to point at the curse, to disguise why he's doing it; but all I see is a human killer with human emotions.'

'Hold it,' said Penny, looking quickly round the church. 'Where's Ian? Her photographer? They were always together.'

'He's not here,' I said. 'We would have found him by now.'

'He swore he'd never let anything happen to Linda,' said Penny. 'Did she say anything about his being here, when she phoned?'

'No,' I said. 'She didn't. Maybe she thought what she knew was so dangerous, she had to send him away.'

'You saw how Ian was,' said Penny. 'You really think he'd just go, and leave her in danger?'

'He would if she told him to,' I said. 'Look, if he turns up later we can ask him. If he doesn't, the killer must have got to him too. Cleaning up loose ends.'

'If he's dead, why isn't he here?'

'Because it got in the way of putting on a show?' I said.

'I really hoped the killings would stop, once Gillian and Tom were married,' said Penny.

'We're missing something,' I said. 'We thought

213

it was down to the curse, or intimidation to prevent the wedding. But the marriage happened anyway . . . but people are still dying. That means the killer is escalating, which means . . . We have to get back to The Swan and move everyone out to Robert's place as quickly as possible. And then turn his house into a fortress. I'm not losing anyone else to this monster.'

Ten

The Curse is Cruel

I raced back through the empty streets, running flat out now there was no one around to see. Penny had to struggle to keep up with me, but I couldn't slow down. Whoever or whatever was behind the murders had to go after Gillian and Tom now. They were the only real targets left. I plunged through the deserted streets until The Swan finally loomed up before me, and I slammed into reception without slowing. Nettie was half-asleep behind her desk, but she snapped to attention as I burst in with Penny right behind me. I strode up to the desk while Nettie was still putting on her professional smile.

'Can I use your phone, Nettie?'

'Of course, dear, help yourself.'

She pushed the phone across the desk to me. I picked it up and then stared at Nettie until she eased out from behind the desk, and disappeared down a side corridor. I couldn't have her listening in, but I just knew she'd find some way to get back at me for my rudeness. I punched a number into the phone, put it to my ear and waited.

'Who are you calling?' said Penny.

'Inspector Godwin,' I said. 'I just hope he's still at the police station.'

'How do you know the number?'

215

'I saw it on the station reception desk.'

'How can you remember something like that?'

'Because unlike most people, I have a memory that works.'

Penny sniffed. 'Then why do you never know where I've left the car keys?'

'Because I'm only human.' The phone kept ringing, but no one was answering. Godwin had to be there, because if he wasn't I had no way of contacting him.

'Why aren't you using your mobile phone?' said Penny.

'Because that phone is only for emergencies,' I said patiently. 'Look, why don't you go through to the bar and tell everyone I'll be there in a minute? Make sure Gillian and Tom are safe, but don't tell anyone what's happened to Linda.'

'Why not?' said Penny. 'Don't they have a right to know that the killer's taken another life?'

'They're scared enough as it is,' I said. 'The last thing they need is another reason to panic.'

Penny nodded reluctantly, and went on through to the bar. Godwin finally answered the phone.

'What do you want? This station is closed till the morning, and I'm very busy.'

'This is Ishmael Jones.'

'Oh hell,' said Godwin. 'Haven't I suffered enough? What is it now?'

'There's been another murder.'

'Are you confessing?'

I told Godwin what had happened to Linda. The way she was killed, and the state of the body.

'Are you sure I'm allowed to get involved with

this?' said Godwin. 'I mean, I'm only a detective inspector.'

'Don't sulk,' I said sharply. 'I need you to go take care of Linda and seal the church off, just in case someone else stumbles across the body.'

'Of course I'll look after Linda,' said Godwin. 'I was at school with her.'

'She told me she knew something important,' I said. 'Some piece of information, or maybe just gossip, that made her a target. Do you have any idea what she might have been talking about?'

'Oh hell . . .' said Godwin, and he paused for a while. I could hear him breathing. When he finally started talking again, he sounded grim and troubled. 'She came to see me. She was desperate for something new about the murder, some obscure detail she could use to impress her editor. And Linda always could twist me around her little finger. I printed out some of the background information I'd found on the police computers, and she took it away.'

'What kind of information?' I said.

'Lots of things! But nothing worth getting killed over. Wait a minute; was Ian in the church? Her cameraman? Is he dead too?'

'There was no sign of him,' I said.

'He'd never have left Linda on her own.'

'Not even if she told him to? If she didn't want to put him in danger too?'

'He might go,' said Godwin, 'but he wouldn't go far.'

'Then you'd better search the area around the church for another body,' I said.

'We have to find this killer,' said Godwin. 'Before he gets to Gillian and Tom. Are you keeping them safe?'

'Anyone who wants to get to them has to go through me,' I said.

'It'll take more than connections to stop a killer like this.'

He hung up on me. I put the phone down and called out to Nettie, to let her know I'd finished and it was all right to come back. She quickly reappeared, smiling determinedly.

'Thanks for the use of the phone,' I said.

'That's all right, dear. I'll just add the cost of the call to Tom and Gillian's bill.' She hesitated, and then looked at me hopefully. 'Will you be going into the town again tonight, dear?'

'Possibly,' I said.

'It's just that if you do, could you keep an eye out for my Albert? He should have been back by now. Of course he prefers to spend his time with his friends, rather than be cooped up here. I know that. But with things the way they are now, I do worry.'

'Of course,' I said.

'I always hoped he'd want to take over the hotel business, once I was gone,' said Nettie. 'But it's really not his thing. So, let him sell it and have some fun with the money. I wish I had.'

I went back to the bar, rehearsing in my head what I was going to say. The moment I walked through the door, the first thing I noticed was the dark mood. No one was talking to anyone, they were just sitting at tables scattered around the bar, looking at their drinks but not touching them. Gillian and Tom were seated side by side, but clearly thinking separate thoughts. Robert was sitting hunched over his table, scowling darkly, and David was off in the far corner, avoiding everyone's eyes and looking sorry for himself. Penny was standing at the bar, where she could keep an eye on all of them, but hurried over to join me the moment I appeared.

'Tom found David passed out in the toilet,' she said quietly. 'Champagne doesn't affect him, my arse. When he was away too long, Tom went looking for him and found him snoring on the floor of the Ladies toilet. They had to break the door in, to get him out. Apparently there was a lot of shouting, and a few unfortunate things were said. So now no one's talking to anyone.'

'Great,' I said. 'Just when I need them to work together.'

'Go ahead and bully them,' said Penny. 'It's for their own good. And you do have a gift for it.'

I let that one pass, and raised my voice to address the bar. 'All right, people, it's time for all of us to move to Robert's house for the rest of the night. Tom, don't check out with Nettie. You can leave that till tomorrow. It's better if everyone thinks you and Gillian are still staying here.'

'We need to go up to our room before we leave,' said Gillian. 'So we can pick up some overnight things.'

'That might be enough to give the game away,' I said. 'You go as you are. You can do without pyjamas or a toothbrush for one night. As far as

Nettie is concerned, we're just popping out for a while. And we can't call for a taxi to take us to Robert's place, because we don't want anyone to know where we're going.'

'I'm starting to remember a message I saw on a T-shirt once,' David said pointedly. *"Just because I'm paranoid it doesn't mean I'm not out to get you".*'

'Ah,' I said. 'But did you really see it, or only think you did?'

'My head hurts,' said David.

'Serves you right,' said Tom.

David glared at him. 'I said I was sorry! It all just got a bit much for me. How many times do I have to apologize?'

'We'll let you know when,' said Tom.

The two men managed a small smile for each other, and then David turned to look at me.

'No taxi . . . We're going to have to walk all the way to the edge of town?'

'If I can manage it, you can,' growled Robert.

'I'm being punished, aren't I?' said David.

'Come on,' I said. 'The sooner we make a start, the sooner it will all be over. On your feet, everyone. And once we're outside I want everyone to stick close together.'

'You want us to form a crocodile?' said David.

'If I thought it would make you any safer I'd put leads round your necks,' I said. 'Come on, people, let's move!'

'Why are you in such a hurry?' said Gillian, as she and Tom got to their feet. 'Aren't we safe here? Has something happened?'

'You'll all be safer when we get to Robert's place,' I said.

That wasn't actually an answer, and everyone knew it.

We made our way back through the lobby, doing our best to look like a cheerful company just stepping out for a little fresh air. We all smiled at Nettie, and she smiled back. I led the way through the front door and then stopped abruptly. There was a taxi parked outside, with Cathy leaning casually against it, looking very pleased with herself. I gestured for everyone to stay where they were, and went to talk to Cathy.

'How did you know . . .?'

'I didn't,' Cathy said cheerfully. 'I've been driving back and forth ever since you told me to stick around. Fortunately, there isn't much call for my services. And by much, I mean any. This town is dead tonight, if you'll pardon the expression. Just as well, given that most of the other taxi drivers called in sick again. Dad is mad as hell. Anyway, I saw you going into the hotel, so I just parked here and waited for you to come out again. Now, where do you want to go?'

'My place,' said Robert, moving in beside me.

'Oh hi, Mr Bergin! Sure, no problem.' And then she looked at the size of the group behind us. 'Though if you're all going, that could mean two journeys. We're going to have a hard time fitting that many people into my cab, no matter how friendly and accommodating they're prepared to be.'

I made it very clear that I didn't want to split

221

up the group, and the others picked up on my sense of urgency. After a certain amount of muttered discussion, Gillian sat on Tom's lap in the back seat, Robert and David crammed themselves in on either side of them, and Penny sat on my lap in the front seat.

'I'm impressed!' said Cathy, as she slipped behind the wheel and cranked up the engine. 'Someone phone the *Guinness Book of Records*; if they can get their hand to their phone. Isn't this cosy? Reminds me of old times, eh, Gilly? All those evenings spent playing Twister with the boys. Drunk, naked, greased . . .'

'Drive the cab,' said Gillian. She looked at Tom. 'Don't ask.'

'I wasn't going to,' said Tom.

'Damn, you've got him well-trained,' said David.

'This isn't a regular fare,' I said to Cathy. 'We need to lie low for a while. Can you not tell your father about this?'

'Oh sure,' said Cathy. 'What's one more reason for him to be mad at me?'

We drove steadily through the town, taking it easy for once, possibly because the taxi was so dangerously overloaded. No one was wearing any seatbelts, because none of us could get to them. I studied the town through the side window. No one was moving in the brightly-lit streets, and there was no other traffic at all. The townspeople were expecting bad things to happen on Gillian and Tom's wedding night, and didn't want the curse to have any reason to look in their direction. I felt even more tense when we left the lights of the town behind, and drove up the lane toward the dark countryside. The taxi's headlight showed the way ahead clearly enough, but the fields on either side remained lost in the night. A darkness so complete anything could be hiding in it. Anything at all.

But we made it all the way to Robert's house without incident, and Cathy brought the taxi to a halt right in front of the door. We all poured out of the taxi like clowns emerging from a circus car, and then spent some time stretching our backs and legs and stamping our feet as we tried to get the circulation moving again. I kept a watchful eye on our surroundings.

'What are you all doing out here?' said Cathy. 'Is it a party? Can I come? I can be the life and soul; ask Gilly.'

'We just felt the need to get away from everything for a while,' I said.

'Are you going to need me again tonight?'

'I doubt it,' I said.

I started to reach into my pocket for the fare, but Cathy stopped me with an upraised hand.

'On the house. Wedding present. And yes, I know, don't tell anyone you're hiding out here.'

She turned the taxi around, and grinned out the side window at Gillian and Tom.

'Have a nice night! Don't do anything I would!'

And then she went speeding off down the narrow lane, laughing raucously, and taking the light with her.

I made everyone stay where they were, standing close together in the gloom; not letting them go inside the house until I'd had a chance to check things out. I made a quick tour of the perimeter, sticking close to the side of the house and straining my eyes against the dark. I moved as quietly as I could, but it was hard not to make a noise in such a quiet setting. I didn't see or hear anything, but I couldn't be sure that was enough. The killer had to be human, but how could he keep appearing and disappearing to do what he did, with no one noticing?

I finally came back to the front of the house, assured everyone that everything was fine, and gestured for Robert to unlock the front door. He soon had the door open and the hall light on, and everyone made small sounds of relief at being able to see clearly again. We all filed quickly into the house, with me bringing up the rear and hurrying them in. I stopped in the doorway for one last look, and the night stared flatly back at me, giving away nothing.

Once we were all inside, Robert made a point of locking the front door, and slamming home a heavy bolt.

'I'm a great believer in bolts,' he said. 'You can pick a lock, but not a bolt.'

'What if we need to leave in a hurry?' said David.

'You won't,' I said. 'That's the point of being here.' I turned to Robert. 'Do any of your windows have locks or bolts?'

'No,' he said, frowning. 'I never thought a time would come when I'd need them. You all go and settle yourselves in the parlour, while I make sure the back door is secure, and then I'll see about rustling up some tea.'

He disappeared toward the back of the house, while I led everyone into the parlour. Its old-fashioned nature helped to make it seem cosy, and welcoming. A safe harbour after a dangerous journey. David and Tom dropped onto the sofa and made themselves at home, while Penny sank gratefully into Robert's chair. I stayed by the door, thinking. Gillian went over to the window and pushed back the curtains to look out at the night, and then pulled them back together again. She stood with her back to the window, her arms folded tightly across her chest, as though to hold herself together. Tom looked at her, but knew better than to say anything. I went over to Gillian.

'Robert told me you weren't happy about being here,' I said quietly. 'Something about an argument with your mother, before she died?'

'No, that's not it,' said Gillian. She kept her voice low. 'That's what I told Dad, but really . . . I always hated this town. Hated being trapped in a place where everybody knew everyone, and you couldn't do anything without everybody knowing all about it. A small town with small lives, and smaller ambitions. I needed to get the hell out of here, so I could reinvent myself as someone else, someone with a future. Small towns don't believe in dreams, or second chances.

'I think I only came back here to be married so I could rub their noses in it. *Look! I got away! I made something of my life in spite of you!* I hated everything about this town, and the quiet

225

secluded life my parents chose for me. I ran away to the big city the moment I was old enough. But any time I came home to visit my mother would only ever see me as who I used to be, the way she wanted me to be. Not the woman I was determined to become. So I stopped coming home. Because coming back felt like giving up. And then she died, before I could prove her wrong.

'And yet here I am again, forced to run home to Daddy just to feel safe, because I can't protect myself. It's bad enough that someone wants to kill me; why did it have to be here?'

She forced a smile. 'Don't tell Dad any of that. He wouldn't understand, and I don't want him upset. For him, this house is full of good memories.'

Robert came back into the parlour, rubbing his hands together with the air of a man who'd finished important work. 'Everything's secure and the kettle's on. Gillian, Tom, you can have my bedroom. It's the biggest.'

'It's also the bed you and Mum used to sleep in,' said Gillian. 'Really not where I want to spend my wedding night, thank you.'

'That only leaves the spare room,' said Robert. 'Where Ishmael and Penny are staying.'

'You're welcome to it,' I said quickly. 'We'll be staying up all night anyway, on guard. It's only a single bed, but very comfortable.'

Tom raised an eyebrow. 'A single bed?'

'Hush, sweetie,' said Gillian. 'We'll manage. You stay here, while I nip upstairs and take a look.'

She hurried out the door before anyone could say anything. Robert shrugged, and went to see about the tea. The rest of us listened to Gillian's footsteps ascending the bare wooden stairs. David heaved himself up off the sofa.

'I think I'll go and help Robert with the tea. See if he's got any decent biscuits anywhere.'

He went out the door. Tom looked at Penny, and then at me. He got to his feet and came over to join me.

'I wonder if I could have a word in private, Ishmael? Just the two of us.'

'I'll take a quick look round the house,' Penny said quickly, getting to her feet. 'Get a feel for the layout.'

Tom waited till she was out the door, and then looked at me reluctantly. 'I have to talk to someone. I can't talk to Gillian's father, and David wouldn't understand . . .'

'I get it,' I said. 'You need another man to talk to, and I'm all that's left. You can tell me anything. I know how to keep a secret.'

'You must have noticed that Gillian and I are a bit on edge, about our wedding night,' said Tom. 'There's a reason for that. More than the obvious ones, I mean. I need you to keep everyone away from us. I know we have to be protected, but we really need some breathing space. You see . . . this really will be the first night we've been together. Gillian is still a virgin. She told me that early on, because it was important to her. Probably because of what she and Cathy got up to, when they were running around together, out of control. It was all about having a good time;

227

until Cathy had her first abortion at sixteen. That made a big impression on Gillian.'

'But, you shared the same room at the hotel,' I said carefully.

'Gillian didn't want anyone to know about us,' said Tom. 'I didn't give a damn, but she can be a bit funny where this town is concerned. All we shared at The Swan was the bed. I mean, yes, we've fooled around some, but we never actually . . .'

'What about you?' I said. 'Are you . . .?'

'No,' said Tom, with as much dignity as he could manage. 'I'm not looking for a pep talk. It's just . . . this night would have been difficult enough for both of us anyway, without all this extra pressure.'

'If you're thinking about putting it off,' I said carefully, 'I'm sorry, but I don't think you can. Getting through the wedding night safely is the only way to make sure the curse doesn't have any hold over you.'

'So much for romance,' said Tom. He made a helpless gesture with both hands, and then smiled bravely. 'I'll just have to be as supportive for her as I can. It doesn't help that we'll be doing it in her parents' house . . . She has issues about this place you wouldn't believe.'

'You just concentrate on Gillian,' I said. 'Don't worry about anything else. None of us will be sleeping tonight; we'll all be standing guard till the morning, to make sure you're safe.'

We both looked round, as David stuck his head through the open doorway.

'Tea is on its way. Everything all right?'

'Sure,' said Tom. 'Everything's fine.'

David wandered in, looked around the room as though surprised to find it so empty, and then came over to join us. He absently removed a stray hair from Tom's collar.

'Relax, Tom,' he said. 'You look fine. Where's Gillian?'

'Still upstairs, checking out the spare room,' said Tom. 'Probably bouncing on the bed to test the springs.'

'I would offer you some helpful advice,' said David. 'But you know the whole boy/girl thing has always been foreign territory to me.'

'I think I can manage without your help, for once,' said Tom. 'I just want to say . . . Thanks for everything, David. You were my best man, all the way.'

David nodded, for once lost for words. He stuck out his hand, and the two men shook hands solemnly.

'I think I'll go up and join Gillian,' said Tom.

'Aren't you going to wait for your tea?' said David.

'No,' said Tom.

'Would you like me to put on some romantic music, help put you in the mood?'

'Really not helping, David.'

'I know,' said David, grinning.

Tom left the room, and we heard him climbing steadily up the wooden stairs.

'This can't be easy for him,' I said. 'Or her.'

'Actors are used to coping with first night nerves,' said David. 'We never let it affect our performance. And anyway, Gillian isn't going to let anything get in the way of getting what she wants. She never does.'

Robert came into the parlour, carrying a silver tray with the best china tea service. I got the feeling it didn't get used much, these days. There was an assortment of traditional biscuits on a plate, and I grabbed a bourbon before they all disappeared. Penny came in after Robert, and nodded quietly to me that everything was quiet and secure. We all sat down, and Robert poured the tea. He took his time doing it, but his hands were perfectly steady. It was good strong tea. For a while, no one said anything.

'There was a time I could have protected my own daughter,' Robert said finally, not looking at anyone. 'When I was in my prime I could have taken on any threat, human or not. You remember, Ishmael.'

'I remember,' I said.

'I hate being old,' said Robert. 'Age takes so much away from you.' He looked at me. 'Do you at least feel old, sometimes?'

'Sometimes,' I said, to keep the peace.

David looked at both of us. He could tell he was missing something, but he could also tell we weren't going to talk about it. He shrugged, and gave his full attention to a custard cream.

And then we all sat up straight and looked around as we heard footsteps approaching, heading up the lane towards the house. We all rose quickly to our feet, putting aside teacups and half-finished biscuits. The footsteps stopped. We all stood very still. There was a knock at the front door.

'Don't answer it!' said David.

'We have to,' said Robert. 'We need to know who it is.'

'Everyone stay put,' I said. 'I'll go.'

I went out into the hall, and Robert was right behind me. I knew there was no point in telling him to go back. I turned on the hall light and went to the front door. I glanced back, and saw Robert had taken up a position at the foot of the stairs. Blocking the way with his body, so anything that wanted to get to Gillian would have to go through him first. Age might have taken his strength, but it hadn't touched his courage. I turned back to the front door, slammed back the bolt, unlocked the door and opened it.

It was Inspector Godwin.

'What are you doing here?' I said.

'Relax,' he said. 'Nothing's happened.' He glanced past me at Robert, standing watching, and moved in a little closer. 'I need to talk to you, Mr Jones. Outside.'

I gestured for him to fall back, and then stepped out into the night. I left the door standing open just a little, to give us some light. I glanced down the lane, to make sure Godwin was on his own. The lane was dark and empty, and the night was very quiet.

'What is it, Inspector?'

'I have something for you.' He pulled a folder from under his arm. 'I walked all the way out here from town, to give you this. It contains every bit of background information I was able to pull up from the police computers, on everyone connected to the family or the wedding . . .'

231

'How did you know I was here?' I said, as I accepted the folder from him.

'Please, I am a detective. You weren't at The Swan, my first choice, so where else could you be? And, I saw Cathy's taxi coming out of this lane. Which doesn't lead anywhere, except to Mr Bergin's house . . .' He scowled at the folder I was holding. 'I still can't believe there's anything in there that could have got Linda killed, but I wanted you to see it. Maybe you can spot something, some connection that I missed . . .'

'Have you been to see Linda?'

'Of course. I couldn't move her, for fear of compromising any evidence. But I have sealed the church door with new crime scene tape. I knew she'd get into trouble some day, chasing after a story too big for her. She always did have more ambition than sense. But . . . You saw how she was killed. Horrible. People around here say the curse is cruel, and I'm starting to think they're right . . .'

'Any sign of Ian?'

'Not so far,' said Godwin. 'But there's only me to look. And I've been on my feet all day . . .'

His voice kept fading out, as though he kept running out of strength.

'You should take a break,' I said.

'How can I? With that vicious bastard still running around loose? I'm all there is, to stand between the town and a killer.'

'With luck, this should all be over by morning,' I said. 'Are you starting to believe in the curse?'

'No. The evil that men do is quite enough for me. Nettie said you all left together. You're hiding out here till the wedding night is over, right? Would you like me to stick around too?'

'Thanks, but no,' I said steadily. 'There are enough people here to keep track of as it is.' *And, I don't want you to see what I might have to do to stop the killer; if it should turn out to be more than human.* 'I'll talk to you again tomorrow.'

Godwin nodded reluctantly, searched for something else to say and couldn't think of anything. He turned abruptly and strode off down the lane. I watched the light from his torch go bobbing off into the night as he headed for town, just to make sure he was leaving, and then I went back inside the house.

I locked and bolted the front door. Robert came forward to join me.

'What did Peter want?'

'He had a file he wanted me to take a look at,' I said.

'Why didn't he come in?'

'He had his reasons. Let's get back to the parlour.'

We went back in, and after I'd explained the reason for Godwin's visit, we all sat down again and settled ourselves. Robert took over his own chair, while Penny and I sat on the sofa, with David perched on the end. Everyone looked curiously at the file I was holding.

'Pity that Peter wouldn't join us,' said Robert. 'We could have used a bruiser like him. You could always rely on Peter to get stuck into anyone who gave Gillian a hard time. One of the few good things about him, when he was at school.'

'The only people I trust are right here in the house,' I said. 'Why complicate things?'

The others went back to their tea and biscuits, with the air of hospital visitors resigned to a long wait. I leafed quickly through the pages in the folder. No real surprises, no big crimes. Just minor convictions and a few past sins.

Robert had several parking offences, and a few speeding tickets, dating back to when he was still driving. Tom and David had several drunk and disorderlies, dating back to their days as students. Gillian had a few run-ins with the police, from going on marches and demonstrations as a teenager in London, with a previous boyfriend. Security had opened a file on her, but all the marching stopped when she broke up with the boyfriend. Cathy had been arrested for assault, after beating up a man in the town centre one night; but the victim dropped all charges before it got to court. There was a handwritten note, presumably from Godwin: *he deserved it.*

The rest was just gossip. Various suggestions as to who Robert really worked for before he retired, all of them reassuringly wide of the mark. A report claiming that Tom had once slipped a laxative into another actor's drink to sabotage his audition, so Tom could get a part he really wanted. David was supposed to have threatened one of Tom's ex-girlfriends to make her go away, because he thought she was a bad influence. And a suggestion he might have done that with other girls he didn't approve of. A report that Gillian had once thrown a drink in the face of a politician who propositioned her in the main House of Commons bar.

I closed the file. Godwin was right; none of this was worth killing over. So what had Linda worked out, what had she thought was so important, that the killer couldn't allow her to talk to me?

David suddenly jumped to his feet and looked about him. 'Did you hear that?'

I threw aside the file and rose to my feet, listening hard. Penny got up to stand beside me, while Robert struggled out of his chair. We all stood very still.

'What did you hear?' I said.

'It was something outside the house.' David was so tense he was actually shaking. 'It sounded like someone moving around.'

Penny looked at me, and I shook my head. I couldn't hear anything.

'Could it be the inspector, come back for something?' said Penny.

'He didn't have any reason to come back,' I said.

'Could it be Ian?' said Penny.

'What would he be doing here?' said Robert.

'Turn out the light, Penny,' I said.

She hurried over to the door, hit the switch, and the room plunged into darkness. I moved over to the window, pushed back the curtains and looked out. I couldn't see far into the dark, but the lane outside the house was definitely empty. The others crowded in behind me.

'Can't see a damned thing,' said Robert.

'I'm not hearing anything,' I said.

'Maybe they've stopped moving,' said David. 'They must know we heard something, because we turned off the light to look. Hold it!' He turned away from the window. 'I can hear something . . . by the front door!'

I ran out of the room and into the hall. The others quickly joined me, and we all stood together in the gloom, staring at the closed front door. I strained my hearing against the quiet, but all I could hear were the rapid heartbeats and strained breathing of the people with me. I moved slowly forward, until I was standing right in front of the door.

'Don't open it!' said David. 'There could be anything out there!'

My hands had clenched into fists so tight they ached. I wanted to open the door, and confront whatever it was, but I couldn't risk letting anything in. I retreated slowly back down the hall to rejoin the others. Not taking my eyes off the front door for a moment. I spoke quietly to Robert.

'Do you have any weapons in the house?'

'No,' he said. 'I thought I'd left that kind of thing behind me, when I retired from Black Heir.'

'I still can't hear anything,' I said.

'If it's an invisible demon, it might be inaudible too,' said Penny.

'Then David wouldn't have been able to hear it at all, would he?' I said.

'I can hear something moving, inside the

236

house!' David said suddenly, his voice rising. 'The back door! It's got in! It's here!'

'It can't have got in!' said Robert.

'I can hear it!' said David. 'Check all the rooms! I'll go upstairs, and make sure they're all right . . .'

'No,' I said sharply. 'You stay right where you are, David.'

He spun round, to stare at me. 'What? Why?'

'Because the killer is inside the house,' I said. 'And it's you, David.'

I moved over to the light switch, and turned it back on. Everyone blinked at the sudden glare except me. Robert was looking at David, Penny was looking at me. I fixed my gaze on David, who was standing very still. His face was completely empty, as though it didn't know what to do.

'You're crazy,' he said.

Robert looked at me. 'Are you sure, Ishmael? David killed the Reverend Allen, and Karen?'

'I wasn't sure until now,' I said. 'You outsmarted yourself, David. We all heard Inspector Godwin walking up the lane to the house, because it's so quiet outside. So why didn't anyone but you hear the movement outside? And then you said something was moving around inside the house. I have exceptional hearing, David. So if I couldn't hear anyone inside the house, that could only mean there was no one. Which meant you were lying. And then you wanted to send us off on a wild goose chase, so you could go upstairs on your own. To get to Gillian and Tom while they were at their most

237

vulnerable. And once I thought that . . . everything just fell into place. All the things I'd noticed, but hadn't put together till now.

'The Reverend Allen was killed by a heavy blow to the back of the neck. And who was the only one of us with a reason to be angry at the vicar? Only you, David. Everyone else went out of their way to say how pleasant he was; but you saw another side of him. Everyone was coming and going at the church hall that evening, so no one paid any attention when you slipped away to confront the Reverend Allen. What did he say to you, David? This old-fashioned vicar who really didn't like gay people?'

'He told me I was an abomination in the eyes of God,' said David. 'That he wouldn't allow the wedding to take place in his church, unless I was replaced as best man. I lost my temper and shoved him. Hard. He fell back and broke his neck against the altar.'

'Hanging him on his own rope was an afterthought,' I said. 'To show what you thought of him, and to point at the curse; so no one would think to blame you. And of course, you knew all about the curse. You'd been reading up on it. But if the vicar's death was an accident . . . why did you kill Karen, and Linda?'

'Linda?' said Robert. 'She's dead too?' He stared at David in horror. 'What have you done, boy . . .?'

David didn't react at all, just kept looking at me.

'I think it was because after the Reverend Allen died, there was serious talk of cancelling the

238

wedding,' I said. 'And you wanted that, David. So you saw your opportunity to make sure the wedding would never happen.'

'Why would I want to do that?' said David.

'Because you love Tom,' I said. 'And you always have. Though he never saw it. And he never would, once he married Gillian. Once Tom left you behind, on your own. Linda got the gossip from Godwin, about you seeing off girls who got too close to Tom. But Gillian was made of harder stuff than that. You thought you'd lost him forever.

'You killed Karen to make it look like the curse was still operating. That it was just too dangerous for Gillian and Tom to get married. You must have been sure another death linked to the curse would be enough to stop the wedding; but it wasn't. And then Linda put two and two together about you, got scared, and called me. You must have overheard me talking to her on the phone at The Swan, leaped to the right conclusion, pretended you were going to the toilet again and left the hotel by the back door. Then you ran through the empty streets to get to the church before I could, killed Linda, and ran back to The Swan. Then all you had to do was pretend to be passed out in the Ladies' toilet to explain your absence. You said champagne didn't affect you, and you were right.

'There were lots of clues that just fell into place, once I knew it had to be you, David. You were the only one of us on your own when Karen was killed. We all had things to do, in the company of others, but you said you were going

239

to a teashop to work on your speech. How did you get Karen to leave the safety of her room, and join you at the church hall? I'm guessing you just phoned her room and said Gillian needed her there. Karen always was a sucker for being needed. And of course, she had no reason to see you as a threat until it was far too late.

'But most of all, it was the manner of the killings that pointed to you. They were all so dramatic, so theatrical, so staged. Just what you'd expect from an actor. And finally, just now, I saw you pluck a stray hair off Tom's collar. A friend wouldn't do something like that, David; it's an intimate act.'

'I don't understand,' said Robert. 'Tom isn't gay.' He looked at David. 'You must have known he was never going to . . .'

'It isn't always about sex!' said David. 'I loved him! We spent years together, as friends, and we were perfectly happy! But then Gillian took him away from me. I never planned any of this, but when I saw my chance I took it. Just once, I wanted what everyone else wants: a happy ever after with the one I love!'

Someone screamed, upstairs. A man's scream, shocked and raw and horrified. I charged up the stairs, taking them two at a time, and was on the landing while the others were still pounding up the steps. I ran to the room at the end. The door was locked. I kicked it in; and there was a huge werewolf, standing over Tom. He lay sprawled and naked on the bed, with bloody claw marks on his chest and a horrified look on his face.

The wolf spun round to face me. Over seven feet tall, standing on two legs, the pointed ears on its lupine head brushed against the ceiling. Its thickly furred body was lean and powerful, the long muzzle was crammed full of teeth, and the paws that were almost hands had vicious claws. Its eyes were yellow as urine, and its scarlet tongue lapped hungrily across jagged teeth as it looked at me. It growled, deep in its throat, warning me not to get between it and its prey. I stepped forward anyway. Tom raised himself painfully on one elbow, and called out desperately.

'Don't hurt her! Please! It's Gillian!'

The wolf crouched, growling threateningly as the others arrived and crammed into the doorway behind me. I stopped where I was and looked at Tom. When I spoke, I kept my voice calm and quiet.

'What happened, Tom?'

'We were in bed,' he said. 'We were . . . And then she changed! She didn't understand what was happening! She didn't know who I was . . . I reached out to her and she attacked me.'

Robert stepped forward into the room, peering over my shoulder. The wolf snarled warningly. Robert stood his ground.

'Gillian; it's me. Your father. Listen to my voice. You know me. Everything's going to be all right, Gillian . . .'

He took another step forward, easing past me, and the wolf went for him. I threw Robert back with a sweep of my arm, and went to meet the wolf. Its clawed hands darted for my throat, but

241

I grabbed hold of both hairy wrists and forced the wolf to a halt. Up close it smelled rank, and feral. It strained against me and I quickly realized I couldn't hold it off for long. It was a lot stronger than me. Robert moved in beside me, and stamped hard on the wolf's left ankle; an old infighting trick. The wolf cried out as its leg buckled. It went down on one knee, and I hit it hard in the side of the head. The blow didn't even jar it. The wolf surged forward again, throwing me off balance. I fell back against Robert, pinning him to the wall. Tom cried out, and the wolf spun round to face him. David threw himself onto its back.

'Get out of here, Tom!' he yelled. 'I'll hold it!'

The wolf spun round and round in the cramped space, trying to throw David off. He closed one arm across the wolf's throat, trying for a strangle hold, but he couldn't make any impression on the wolf's thick neck muscles. It reached back with one overlong arm, and David cried out horribly as heavy claws sank deep into his shoulder. Blood spurted, and he lost his grip. The wolf bent sharply forwards, and David flew over its lowered head and slammed into the wall. He hit hard enough to drive all the breath out of him, and dropped to the floor. The wolf lashed out, and vicious claws ripped half his guts away.

I pushed Robert out of the room, and Penny grabbed him, to hold him up. I yelled at the wolf, and it spun round to face me. Blood dripped thickly from its claws. And I knew it would kill me, kill all of us; because I wasn't strong enough to stop it. Unless I released the only monster powerful enough to do the job. My other self; my alien self. I knew if I did that it might not want to go back again. It might decide its time had come, to take over my life. To throw me off, like an old coat it didn't need any more. But I had no choice. I had to save these people from the wolf.

I spared one last glance at Penny. 'Keep everyone back. And run, if you have to.'

'Ishmael . . .?'

'Whatever happens, Penny. Remember I loved you.'

I sent a silent prayer to my other self. *Stop Gillian, but don't kill her. Don't kill anyone. Please.* And then I just stopped fighting, and let it out.

Something manifested in the room. I wasn't there any more, just a thought hovering on the air, watching. Something new was standing in the room where I used to be. I couldn't seem to grasp what it was; as though human eyes weren't enough to make sense of it. Robert and Penny cried out and fell back, unable even to look at it. The wolf fell back a step, shaken and confused, and then it threw itself at the alien with clawed hands and gaping jaws.

A misshapen hand snapped out and grabbed the wolf by the throat, stopping it dead in mid air. The wolf fought furiously against the inhuman grip, but couldn't break free. It howled with rage, lashing out with its clawed hands, but couldn't reach the alien. And then the misshapen hand closed abruptly, shutting off the wolf's air. It thrashed wildly, and then passed out. The wolf hung limply from the alien's hand. My other self studied the wolf for a long moment; and then the hand opened, and the wolf crashed to the floor. By the time it got there, it had turned back into Gillian. She lay there, naked and unconscious, breathing harshly. Tom forced himself over the side of the bed and dropped onto the floor beside her. He took her in his arms, and glared defiantly at the alien.

'Don't you touch her!'

And just like that, the alien was gone. It disappeared back inside me, like slipping on an old familiar coat you've grown fond of, and I was standing in the room again. The alien could have stayed, but it chose not to. It could have killed Gillian, and everyone else, but it didn't want to. It could have taken over my life and forgotten me, but it didn't. My alien self went back to sleep again, of its own free will. And I thought . . . perhaps my original self isn't as bad, or as alien, as I always thought it was. Perhaps there was hope, for the future.

The strength went out of my legs, and I sat down hard on the edge of the bed. Penny hurried into the room and sat on the bed next to me, putting an arm round my shoulders. I leaned against her.

'You didn't run,' I said.

'Why would I run?' she said. 'It was only you.'

Tom checked Gillian was all right, leaned her back against the wall, and then crawled painfully over to David. Blood was still pouring out of the awful wound in his side, but it was beginning to slow. His breathing was shallow, his eyes only just open. He managed a small smile for Tom, who smiled back.

'I'm sorry, Tom,' said David. 'I killed all those people. I'm so sorry.'

'Why?' said Tom. 'Why did you do it?'

'Because I loved you. Because I wanted to be with you, always. Don't hate me, Tom.'

'You're my best friend,' said Tom. 'And you always will be. But you're an idiot.'

'I know that,' said David.

And then he died.

Eleven
The Real Bergin
Family Curse

Some hours later, after we'd all got as much sleep or rest as we were going to, we gathered together again in the parlour. It was morning, and the room was full of light. Everyone seemed to feel a little better, now the long night was over. Tom and Gillian sat together on the sofa, clinging to each other like children. Gillian was still in shock, but her hard-headedness was holding her together. It helped that Tom was right there with her, despite everything he'd been through. Now and again he'd scratch at the bandages under his shirt that Gillian had put in place. She wouldn't let anyone else touch him. Robert sat beside them, doing his best to be supportive without intruding. Penny sat in the big chair, watching me stand by the window. Waiting patiently for me to make the big speech and explain everything. I hoped I'd got it all right. I'd been working on it for hours.

'There really was a Bergin curse,' I said finally. 'But it had nothing to do with the original wedding murders, or any witch. There were a number of werewolf killings reported in and around Bradenford at the same time. Someone in the Bergin family must have been a shape-changer. And was either killed or imprisoned, given that the killings suddenly stopped. The family must have discovered that the wolf gene was only carried on the female side of the family, and that the first change was triggered by the passion of a wedding night. The confused wolf bride would lash out at whoever they were with, killing the groom. As Gillian almost did with Tom. That's why the brides either killed themselves afterwards, or went mad. And that is the Bergin family curse.

'They made up the story about the witch, to put off any more Bergin daughters from getting married. Blaming the dead grooms on an invisible demon, because no one ever saw who killed them. The story existed to hide the family's shame. They couldn't have anyone knowing that the very respectable Bergin line was connected to shape-changing and murder. Given that there were no Bergin daughters for a considerable time, I have to wonder whether they just killed any female babies, to try and stamp out the gene . . . But then there was the big break up in the family, in the nineteenth century, when whole sections stopped talking to each other; and the secret of the curse was lost and forgotten.

'By the time Gillian appeared, the werewolf gene had become so rare it was almost recessive. No one else in the family had changed shape for years, so the curse became just a legend. But somehow the gene is strong in Gillian.'

I exchanged a glance with Robert. It was always possible some of the strange things he'd been exposed to in his time at Black Heir might be responsible. But that was a talk for another time.

'So I could change shape again,' said Gillian. 'Every time we . . .'

'Not necessarily,' I said quickly. 'You were caught by surprise, last night. Now you know, you can learn to control it. Keep the wolf at bay. It is possible. Trust me, I know.'

Tom frowned. 'I was pretty out of it, but I'm sure I saw you . . .'

'Best not to think about it,' I said. 'Let's just say, we all have our secrets.'

Tom nodded. 'Like poor David.'

'I liked him,' said Gillian.

'Everybody did,' said Tom.

'I know people who know people,' said Robert. 'They can help you with this, Gillian.'

'I'd like that,' said Gillian. 'Though we are going to have to talk about exactly who you used to work for.'

Robert nodded. 'It's past time.' He looked at me. 'What are we going to do about David?'

'We let him take the blame for everything,' I said. 'The authorities don't need to know about the curse. David lost his mind and killed three people, and then took his own life. They'll settle for that.'

'So we're throwing David to the wolves,' said Tom. He smiled briefly. 'He'd like that.'

We all looked round as we heard a car approach the house. I looked out the window, in time to see Cathy's taxi pull up outside. Detective Inspector Godwin was sitting in the front seat beside her. I told the others to stay put, and went out into the hall. There was a knock on the front door. I opened it, and there were Cathy and Godwin.

'Morning!' Cathy said cheerfully. 'I found him wandering around last night, looking lost. So I took him home and banged his brains out all night. He's a lot better now. But he insisted on coming out here, first thing.'

'And now I have some work to take care of,' said Godwin. 'So if you wouldn't mind . . .'

Cathy shrugged easily. 'Oh sure. I'll wait in the taxi. Don't be long, darling. I haven't finished with you yet.'

She went back to her taxi. I invited Godwin into the hall, and closed the door.

'I won't take you through to see the others,' I said. 'They're all recovering, after the events of the past few days.'

'But is it over?' said Godwin. 'Is everything all right now?'

'Yes,' I said. 'You don't need to worry about the curse any more, and the town can get back to normal. We now know who was responsible for the killings. It was David Barnes.'

'The best man?' said Godwin. 'Why?'

I gave him the short explanation, just enough to make sense. He didn't need to know about werewolves and curses.

'David killed himself last night,' I said. 'Self-mutilating, out of guilt and remorse. The body is upstairs, waiting to be removed.'

'I'll take care of that,' said Godwin. 'Apparently the big chemical fire is finally under control, so I should be getting reinforcements any time now.'

'And you can take all the credit for finding the murderer,' I said.

Godwin looked at me sharply. 'Why?'

'Because officially, I was never here,' I said. 'It's all yours.'

'You really think my superiors will accept I did it all on my own?' said Godwin.

'Robert will back you up,' I said. 'He has connections; remember?'

We didn't actually share a smile; but we came close.

'I almost forgot,' said Godwin. 'I found Ian. He was working in the *Echo*'s archives, on Linda's orders. He had no idea what had happened, until I told him. He's really broken up over her death, but taking some comfort from the fact that she cared enough about him to keep him out of harm's way.'

I opened the front door for him, and we went outside. Cathy yelled to Godwin from the taxi.

'Come on, lover!'

Godwin looked at me. 'She's scary, but fun.'

He went to join her. I shut the front door. Penny came into the hall to find me.

'We dealt with more than one curse, on this case,' she said. 'The Bergin curse; and yours.'

'The long night is finally over,' I said. 'I'm not as scared of who I used to be, as I used to be.'

'Whoever you are, you're still you,' said Penny.

'Let's hope so,' I said.

Robert came out into the hall. 'So, I suppose you'll be off now?'

'I've done all I can,' I said. 'And I'm really not one for long goodbyes.'

Robert shook my hand firmly. 'Thanks for coming.'

'What are old friends for?' I said. I looked at him. 'You saw me change . . . So now you know.'

'Me?' said Robert, innocently. 'I never saw a damned thing.' He grinned. 'But I always knew there was something rum about you.'